MW00477254

JOY

JOY

A Folly Beach Christmas Mystery

BILL NOEL

Enigma House Press

Also by Bill Noel

Folly Beach Mysteries

Folly

The Pier

Washout

The Edge

The Marsh

Ghosts

Missing

Final Cut

First Light

Boneyard Beach

Silent Night

Dead Center

Discord

Dark Horse

The Folly Beach Mystery Collection

Copyright © 2018 by Bill Noel

All rights reserved.

No part of this book may be reproduced in any form or by any electronic
or mechanical means, including information storage and retrieval systems,
without written permission from the author, except for the use of brief
quotations in a book review.

Cover photo and design by Bill Noel

Author photo by Susan Noel

ISBN: 978-1937979287

Enigma House Press
Goshen, Kentucky
www.enigmahousepress.com

Chapter 1

Barb Deanelli was waiting for me in front of her condo building on West Arctic Avenue. It was a little after sunrise on a cold, mid-December morning, and she had on black skinny jeans, a black down jacket with a texture that looked like bubble-wrap packing material, black boots and a black wool beanie cap. She looked like someone planning to break in someone's second-story window.

Barb folded her five-foot-ten-inch trim frame into the front seat of my car and gave me a peck on the cheek. She was sixty-four years old, three years younger than me, yet looked much younger.

"You look more ready to climb Mt. Everest than hunt shark teeth," I said and leaned closer to receive another kiss.

I was rewarded with an eye roll from the woman I'd been dating for six months. "After last-night's storm, I didn't know what to expect. Besides, the wind's kicking up and from previous trips to the County Park, I knew that there was nothing to block it from chilling my bones."

The Folly Beach County Park anchors the west end of the small South Carolina barrier island and is a mile and a half from Barb's condo. The park doesn't open to vehicles until ten, so I navigated the turnaround in front of the locked gate and moved to the nearest spot where I could pull off the road and park.

Barb was wiser than I was since I didn't have a down coat and had to get by with a lightweight jacket over a long-sleeve denim shirt. I'd never admit that I was cold and on my way to freezing in the brisk wind.

The park consists of more than a hundred acres of mainly flat, sandy terrain, and its beach covers more than four-thousand feet of ocean frontage. There's a picnic area, boardwalks, showers, dressing areas, and restrooms, but we appeared to be the only humans making our way from the deserted parking area to where she hoped to find shark teeth along the receding tideline.

"Tell me again why you decided to drag me out here this morning," I said as I put my arm around her waist to help block the wind. Block it from me, not from her.

"One of my customers, Michelle, makes shark teeth jewelry. I asked where she bought the teeth and she said she found them on the beach, and the best time to find them is after a storm stirs up the surf and extracts them from deeper water. I suppose I've led a sheltered life and didn't know that you could find them here."

"Thinking about making and selling jewelry in the store?"

Barb moved to Folly a year ago from Pennsylvania and opened a used bookstore on the town's main drag.

"No, it takes more patience than I have. I told Michelle I'd carry hers. She did pique my interest enough to ask where she found the teeth. She said anywhere along the beach, and the County Park was a good location, especially before others traipsed along the waterline and grabbed them." She waved her arms toward the ocean. "And, here we are."

Residents and visitors spend hours scouring the beach hunting the teeth that can date to prehistoric times, but in the decade that I'd lived here, I'd never found any. Someone once told me that you don't find shark teeth, they find you. Fortunately, no teeth still attached to a shark have found me, nor have any teeth from their ancestors. I didn't know about shark teeth, but yesterday and last night's tumultuous storm brought some of the largest waves I'd seen in years. Regardless, it was fun spending the morning with Barb.

Then it ceased being fun.

Barb pointed to something at the shoreline a hundred yards in front of us. It looked like a surfboard with someone splayed out on top. My hunch was confirmed as we got closer. The surfboard was barely out of the water and the body of a woman was partially on the board with her arms wrapped around it. Long, black hair either flecked with gray or mixed with sand was spread out and covered part of the white board. She had on tan khaki slacks, a red sweatshirt, and was barefoot. I wasn't optimistic about her being alive since the water temperature was in the low fifties and prolonged exposure to it could be fatal. The top of her sweatshirt was dry, but the lower half was wet as were her slacks.

I bent down to feel for a pulse when her left hand grabbed my wrist. The sudden movement startled me, and I fell backward in the damp sand. She let go and pushed up off the board before falling back. Barb moved to the other side of the board, knelt, and whispered something to the woman. The sky was getting lighter, and I noticed the woman's arms shivering.

I removed my jacket and covered her back. Barb laid her heavier jacket over the woman's legs before wrapping her arms around her to provide body heat.

I leaned back and punched 911 on my phone and told the dispatcher where we were and what we found. I suggested that along with medical help, she send the police. I didn't know what had happened but was confident that it wasn't a surfing accident.

Barb was talking to the woman who'd turned on her side and faced my friend. A good sign.

The screaming siren of a police cruiser could be heard a few blocks away, and the distinct sound of one of the city's fire engines followed the cruiser. Help was on the way. The car's siren shut off, and it took another minute for its occupant to open the park's gate and continue to the parking area near where we were huddled.

"Chris Landrum, is that you?" yelled a Public Safety Officer, the official name of Folly's police officers.

I turned toward the voice and recognized Officer Allen Spencer. I'd met him shortly after he and I arrived on Folly ten years ago. At the time, he was in his mid-twenties, six-feet-tall, and at least thirty pounds lighter. We crossed paths often and had a good relationship.

"Allen," I said and stood to shake his hand.

We shook, and he nodded toward Barb. "Ms. Deanelli."

Barb acknowledged the new arrival and Officer Spencer shifted his attention to the person Barb had her arm around and who was sitting on the surfboard. Spencer saw how much she was shaking and added his heavy jacket to mine and Barb's.

The fire engine pulled beside Spencer's vehicle and two firefighters hurried over. One carried a heavy blanket and wrapped it around the woman. The other firefighter, who on Folly doubled as certified EMT, started taking the woman's vitals.

She was in good hands, so I stepped away from the medical team. Spencer followed and looked up and down the shore and then toward the parking area. "Chris, what happened?"

I said I had no idea and this was how Barb and I'd found her. He asked why we were here, and I shared Barb's story about hunting shark teeth. One of the EMTs returned Barb's coat and offered me my jacket.

Spencer watched him go back to his patient and asked me, "Did she say anything?"

"She mumbled something to Barb, but I didn't hear what it was."

Barb was standing back and watching the EMTs work on the woman. Spencer waved her over and asked her the same thing he'd asked me.

"She asked two questions. She said, 'Where am I?' I told her on Folly Beach." Barb looked back at the woman and shook her head.

I said, "The second question?"

Barb looked at Spencer. "She asked, 'Who am I?'"

Chapter 2

The sun had begun warming the air while Barb, Officer Spencer, and I stood back and watched the EMTs load their patient in the ambulance that had arrived from nearby Charleston ten minutes after the first responders from the fire department. The three of us moved to the surfboard to see if it held any clues to what had happened.

Spencer flipped the board over and glanced at its underside. "This isn't a crime scene, so it doesn't matter if I disturb it," he said, more to himself than to Barb and me.

I knew as much about surfboards as I knew about the Harappan civilization. "Learn anything?"

"Not really. It's a Channel Islands New Flyer. Popular and common. Board of the year a few years back."

Officer Spencer spent many off-duty hours sitting on a surfboard waiting for the perfect wave, so I wasn't surprised with his knowledge of the vehicle that transported our mysterious lady to shore. I suspected that's where his knowledge about the event ended.

The first firefighter to the scene had loaded his equipment on his vehicle and came over to the three of us.

Spencer said, "Len, is she going to be okay?"

"I didn't see any signs of physical trauma. She has hypothermia and if you hadn't found her when you did, she might not have made it. Did you notice the red marks around her ankles?"

I said I had.

The firefighter, whom I'd never met before today, said, "It's not uncommon to see something similar caused by a surf leash attached to the ankle. Never around both ankles. She also has marks around her wrists."

"Think she was restrained?" I said.

"That'd be my guess. Don't hold me to it. It's for someone else to determine. Gotta get back to the station."

Spencer said, "Len, before you go, did she say anything about who she is or how she got here?"

"Nothing that made sense. Her speech was slurred, and she didn't appear to know where she was or why. Allen, don't read too much into it. Those are symptoms of hypothermia. She'll probably be fine in a few hours."

"Did you ask her name?"

He nodded. "She couldn't remember."

Len repeated that he had to get back to the station and walked away as a silver Ford F-150 XLT pickup truck slid to a stop in the sand behind Spencer's cruiser. Cindy LaMond was named Director of Folly Beach's Department of Public Safety two years ago, and I'd known her since she joined the police force six years before that. She was a good friend and married to Larry LaMond, owner of Pewter Hardware, Folly's only hardware store.

The five foot three, well-built bundle of energy didn't

waste time getting to us. In her endearing style, she said, "Hi Barb, what's that old fart Landrum dragged you into this time?"

I didn't recall dragging Barb into this or similar situations, but I'd inadvertently been ensnared in a few horrific situations since retiring on Folly after a peaceful, a.k.a. boring life as a bureaucrat in a large insurance company in Kentucky.

Barb didn't know Cindy as well as I did, but knew her enough to ignore her comment. "Hi, Chief. Chris and I were looking for shark teeth and instead found a damsel in distress."

"Crap, Barb, you're beginning to sound like the old fart." The chief turned to me, "Okay, spill it. What in the hell have you stepped in now?"

We shared everything, which wasn't much, about what we'd found.

Cindy gazed out to sea, and said, "My highly trained police brain tells me that the person who rode in on this board didn't surf from Wales. Any boats out there earlier? Any evidence she was at the park before ending at water's edge?"

"No and no," I said.

Spencer said, "It's possible she came from Kiawah."

Kiawah was another barrier island, and a gated resort fewer than two miles across the Folly River and the Stono Inlet from the County Park.

Cindy sighed. "It's also possible she was dropped out of a space ship and landed on our lovely slice of earth. Officer Spencer, contact the powers that be on Kiawah and see if they have any missing person reports. I'll do the same here."

I said, "Anything I can do, Chief?"

"Yes, you and the lovely lady standing beside you, the one I can't figure a reason in the world why she'd want to hang around with you, continue your search for shark teeth." She snapped her fingers. "Oh yeah, one other thing. Don't, that's do not, get the slightest inkling to butt in police business."

"Cindy——"

She interrupted, "I know, I know." She waved her hand in my face. "There's a better chance of you sprouting wings and flying to the Bahamas than minding your own business. Give it a try, for once."

"Of course, Cindy."

If she noticed my crossed fingers, she didn't let on.

Barb and I made our way to the car and were savoring heat pouring out of the vents. Our jackets were damp from covering the woman and Barb's teeth chattered.

"What do you think happened?" she asked as she rubbed her hands together in front of the vent.

"I don't think she started from the County Park, so Kiawah or from a boat seem like the most logical explanation. Another possibility is that she drifted to the ocean from either the Stono or the Folly River which means she could have gone in the water from several places. I hope someone reports her missing. That'd answer most of the questions."

"Hypothermia can cause temporary memory loss. If the EMT is correct, there's a good chance she could answer questions fairly soon."

"I hope so. One thing I'm certain of is that she didn't decide to go surfing dressed like that. Something happened, something bad."

"I don't disagree." She hesitated, and then in a lower

voice said, "Are you going to follow Cindy's advice and leave whatever's happened to the police?"

Barb was aware of my knack of accidentally stepping in piles of problems, occasionally including murder. Less than a year ago, and with the aid of a few friends, I'd helped catch a killer who was seconds away from ending Barb's life.

"I'll try."

She smiled. "Thanks for not lying and saying that you wouldn't get involved. I'll take an *I'll try*."

I returned her smile and said what I wanted to do now was get her home so she could get in warm clothes and so I could do the same. I let her out at the gate to her condo complex and she left me with, "My next search for shark teeth will be at Mr. John's Beach Store."

I thought it was an excellent idea.

———

My best friend since I arrived on Folly, correction, my best friend ever, is Charles Fowler. We met during my first week here and it didn't take long to learn that he and I were as different as a blue jay was to a blue whale. Charles retired to Folly at the age of thirty-four. Since then and now, as he approached his sixty-fifth birthday, he'd never held a steady job. He picked up enough money to live modestly in a tiny apartment by providing an extra set of hands for local contractors, helping restaurants clean during vacation season, and delivering packages for our friend Dude Slone, owner of the surf shop. I'd spent those same years working in boring jobs while living a boring existence. Charles has quirks too numerous to list. Despite our many differences, we overcame the law of averages, and became closer than brothers. One of his quirks should be mentioned. If I learned something he'd consider interesting, such as discovering a beached lady at the County Park and didn't share it with him in the first seconds after learning it, I would be subjected to a glare, reprimands, and being chastised unmercifully.

I wasn't in the mood to be harassed and called him on my way home.

"Charles, good morning. I just left the County Park with Barb where we found an unconscious woman on——"

"Meet me at the Dog in fifteen minutes."

He'd hung up. It'd been more than a few seconds since we'd found the woman.

Chapter 3

The Lost Dog Cafe was less than a block off Center Street, the figurative center of commerce on the half mile wide, six-mile long island. I and many others consider it the best breakfast spot on Folly. My kitchen was used as often as a wood pencil in the BIC factory, so I'd spent countless mornings enjoying a warm breakfast, the company of my favorite server Amber, and conversations with various friends and acquaintances. It was named the Lost Dog Cafe, although there were approximately a zillion photos of dogs, none of them lost, attached to most every vertical surface in the restaurant. Its two outdoor patios were dog friendly and often occupied by more than one canine. Festive Christmas lights were strung around the railing around the front patio.

"Morning, Chris," Amber said as she met me at the door. "Your regular table?"

Amber was the one person on Folly who I'd known longer than Charles—two days longer. She was on the verge of her fiftieth birthday, five foot five inches tall, with long auburn hair, often tied in a ponytail while she was at work. She's funny, insightful, and one of Folly's rumor-collecting-champions. She and I had dated for a while and after that remained good friends. December was one of the few times of the year when the Dog wasn't packed and my favorite table along the back wall was vacant. I told her yes to my seating preference.

She pointed to the table and said, "Go ahead. I'll grab your water."

Two city councilmembers, Marc and Houston, were seated at their preferred table in the center of the room. They had been on the council as long as I'd been on Folly and weren't in danger of losing their elected positions anytime soon. Another position they weren't in danger of losing was as the town's unofficial gossips, especially Marc. To stretch the tree falling in the forest question, if something happened on Folly and Marc didn't know about it, did it really happen?

I said hi to the councilmembers, received pleasant grins, and from Marc, "Hey, Chris, what's new?"

I wasn't ready to throw the events from the County Park into the gossip mill. "Not much, how about you, Marc?"

"Same old, same old."

I smiled and nodded at the phrase I never understood since I wouldn't have a way of knowing what the same was with Marc, much less how the same had happened again. The smile was because I was surprised that he hadn't heard about the woman. I didn't have time to savor that knowledge since Charles barreled through the door and pointed at the table with his handmade wooden cane that he carries for no apparent reason. I nodded again, this time without the smile, and he made a beeline to the table.

At five-foot-eight, Charles was a couple of inches shorter than me and unlike my balding head, his graying hair always appeared to be in search of a comb. He wore a long-sleeved, gray and crimson, Washington State University sweatshirt, jeans that were too large, a canvas Tilley hat, and three days of unshaven stubble.

He slid in the booth before I could get there, smiled, and said, "What took you so long to get here?"

I didn't take the bait but did take a sip of water from a Ball jar that Amber had slid in front of me.

"Spill it."

I figured he meant the story about the woman and not the water, so in a voice low enough not to reach the gossip-gathering ears of Marc and Houston, began rehashing the trip to the County Park. As with sharing most stories with Charles, I didn't get far before he interrupted.

"Who was she? Did her sweatshirt have a logo on it? Is she going to be okay? Did she have a dog with her?"

"Don't know. No. Don't know. No."

"I'm confused."

I'm usually the one with that feeling. "About what?"

"Which question I asked first?"

Amber returned with water for Charles, one of her endearing smiles, and the question, "What can I get you for breakfast?"

I said, "French toast."

"Lordy, Chris. One of these days you're going to order something different and my little-ole heart won't be able to take the shock."

Charles patted her on the arm. "Don't worry, Miss Amber, your heart's safe. And, if you're interested, I'll have the Loyal Companion."

She ruffled his unruly hair and said that she was always interested in him, pivoted and headed to the kitchen to order my French toast and bacon and eggs for Charles, a.k.a. the Loyal Companion.

"Okay," Charles said, "I'll start over. Are you sure she didn't tell you her name?"

I shook my head.

"I hate calling her *the woman*. Let's go with Jane Doe."

I nodded.

"Could Jane have gone in the water at the Park?"

"It's possible, although unlikely. There was nothing nearby that indicated that she'd been there before she washed up."

"No one goes surfing in khakis and a sweatshirt."

I didn't think that astute observation merited comment. I waited for him to continue.

"If Jane fell off a boat, she wouldn't have landed on a surfboard. Dressed like she was, it's unlikely that she would've willingly stepped in the water off Kiawah or somewhere back in the river. You're sure there was no evidence that someone smacked her in the head and dumped her in the Atlantic?"

"Sure, no. There was nothing obvious."

"She could've been drugged."

"It'll be up to the docs and the police to figure what happened."

"Chris, I was thinking."

Always scary when it came to Charles. I took a deep breath and said, "What?"

"Luck, karma, fate, predestination, whatever led you to Jane. She could've died if you weren't there. You saved her, so it's destined that you must figure out what happened."

"Charles, you know—"

He waved his hand in my face. "Here's the best part. I'll take time out of my busy schedule to help. Great news, right?"

For reasons unknown to anyone, Charles had decided a few years back that he was a private detective. Did he have a law enforcement background? Not unless you count being on weed patrol when he worked for a landscaper fifty years ago in his hometown of Detroit. Did he have private detective training? Absolutely not. Was he a licensed private detective? Nope. He was, however, a voracious reader with an apartment filled with more books than a Barnes & Noble store. He'd claimed to have read every mystery novel written since Gutenberg invented the printing press. That was an exaggeration, although not by much.

"That's a kind offer, considering how busy you are." I hoped he grasped my sarcasm since he didn't work and from what I could tell, had a blank calendar.

"Where do we begin?"

I sighed. "Charles, we don't know anything about her or what happened. I'm sure Chief LaMond will solve it."

He grinned. "See, Chris, Cindy LaMond is your friend. You found Jane. Your involvement is meant to be." He picked my cell phone off the table and handed it to me. "Go ahead, call and see what she's learned and tell her we're on the case."

That wasn't going to happen for more reasons than I could count. "Charles, she hasn't had time to learn anything. I suspect Jane is still at the hospital being evaluated."

"You're right again. Call me this afternoon after you talk to Cindy."

If I wanted to eat in peace, I knew what I had to say. "Sure."

Charles didn't get a chance to pin me down on what time I'd call him. He looked up and saw Burl Iven Costello standing by our table with a smile on his face.

"Good morning Brother Charles and Brother Chris," said the five-foot-six-inch tall, portly man with a milk-chocolate colored mustache who was standing beside the table.

Burl, known to most as Preacher Burl Ives Costello, arrived on Folly two years ago after founding and for several reasons closed churches in Mississippi, Florida, and Indiana. He began First Light, a non-denominational church that met most Sundays on the beach near the Folly Beach Fishing Pier. I'd become better acquainted with him when he became the prime suspect in the murder of two of his followers. Charles and I helped the police catch the killer when he tried to add Preacher Burl to his list of victims.

"Join us Preacher," Charles said, as he slid to the end of the seat to make room for the newcomer.

"If you don't mind."

He slid in beside Charles, not waiting to hear if we minded. He looked around the room and turned to Amber who was quick to the table to see what he needed. Charles told him to order anything he wanted because I was picking up the check. Charles was in the holiday spirit with my wallet. Burl said coffee was all since he'd had breakfast.

"Preacher," Charles said, "any trouble with the nativity this year?"

First Light Church had an impressive nativity scene squeezed on a narrow piece of land between the Folly Beach Post Office and Pewter Hardware Store. Last Christmas someone stole a valuable, hand-carved baby Jesus from the display, nearly sucking the Christmas spirit out of the island. A miracle in the form of two teenagers averted a disaster by finding the missing figurine Christmas Eve.

"Brother Charles, it's been perfect this year. Praise the Lord." He smiled. "Baby Jesus won't be making an appearance until Christmas Day and will be under the watchful eyes of members of our flock."

"Wise move," I said, and since he wasn't here to eat, asked, "What brings you out this morning?"

"Excellent question, Brother Chris. I was looking for Brother Taylor, one of my residents."

The residence Burl referred to was Hope House, which loosely could be described as a halfway house that the preacher had started nine months ago. A wealthy and generous member of First Light donated a six-bedroom house on East Erie Avenue under the condition that Burl would rent to people he felt needed the assist to get back to productive members of the community. Rent was based on ability to pay and ranged from zero to a few hundred dollars a month, with most residents near the zero end of the scale.

Charles looked around the room. "Don't suppose he's here?"

"No, Brother Charles."

"Why are you looking for him?" I asked.

"I learned of an outstanding job that I believe his skills would make him a perfect candidate."

"That's great, Preacher. How's the house doing?"

"Most of my prayers have been answered, although we've had a few challenges," Burl said, and nodded like he was praying. He then turned to me and smiled. "Our benefactor said that the house needed a couple of cosmetic improvements. I didn't realize a new electrical system qualified as cosmetic." Burl chuckled. "At least when the power was off, the residents didn't know that the air conditioner was also, how shall I put it, under the weather."

"What's going to happen?" Charles asked.

Burl looked toward the ceiling like he was checking with God for an answer. "Brother Charles, I'm leaving it in the hands of the Lord."

"Preacher, I don't think—"

"Worry not, Brother Charles, the Lord already sent an electrician and an HVAC specialist to address the issues. The Lord sent them, and Brother Edward sent a check to cover the expenses."

"Brother Edward?" I said.

"Edward Bancroft, the wonderful man who donated the house."

"That's great," Charles said. "How many residents are there?"

"Four, each is blessed with a private room although two of the rooms are so large that we could put two people in each if need be." Burl glanced over my shoulder. "Ah, there's my resident. I would like to stay longer but feel the necessity of sharing with him the good news about the job." He stood, said, "May you have a blessed day," and headed to the door to meet his resident.

Charles watched Burl put his arm around the shoulder of the man as he escorted him to an empty table. He then turned to me and glanced at his wrist where most people wore a watch. His was bare. "Isn't it time for you to call Cindy and find out about Jane Doe?"

I took a sip of coffee, regretted it immediately since it had turned cold, stared at Charles, and said, "No. She hasn't had time to learn more than she would've known fifteen minutes ago when I told you that I'd call her this afternoon."

Charles sighed. "Worth a try. You're going to call me as soon as you hang up with the Chief?"

"Yes, oh patient one."

———

It was two hours later, and if I didn't call the Chief soon, Charles would be on my doorstep wondering why I hadn't let him know what she said.

"What took you so long to pester me about Joyce?" Cindy LaMond said when she answered the phone.

I would have preferred something along the lines of, "*Hi, Chris. How are you this afternoon? How may I help you?*" I also would have preferred to be twenty pounds lighter, thirty years younger, and have a full head of hair. The odds were equal for any of those events happening.

"Who's Joyce?"

"How quickly you forget, Mr. Senior Citizen. You found her this morning."

"The person we found said she didn't know her name. Is her memory back?"

"Nope."

I sighed. "How do you know her name's Joyce?"

"Superb detective work, an incredibly high level of training and experience, use of all of my Super Chief skills."

"And?"

"And, Joyce was printed with a laundry marker pen on the label in her sweatshirt."

"Wow. No wonder you're Chief."

"True, oh so true, Mr. Senior Citizen."

"Did your superpowers tell you if Joyce was her first or last name?"

"First, I assume. Who ever heard of Joyce as a last name?"

I wasn't a big reader and had seldom paid attention in literature class in school, but it didn't take a scholar to have heard of James Joyce. I shared that tidbit.

"How about anyone with that last name in our lifetime?"

"None I can think of."

"Then I'm sticking with it as her first name."

"Cindy, has she said anything about what happened?"

"Very little. She thinks she remembers being on a boat, a storm, and then in the water clutching the surfboard. Her next memory is of some old geezer staring at her."

"Old geezer?"

She shrugged. "I added that part. Anyway, she claims she doesn't know anything else."

"Had she been injured? I didn't see any sign of physical injury."

"She's at the hospital getting a complete checkup. They're planning on having a head-doc talk with her to see if she understood what happened. They'll hold her overnight and if nothing pops up, release her in the morning."

"Then what?"

"Then I'll see if her memory is back. I'm having my guys check if there's a missing person report matching her description."

"And, then what?"

"Heck if I know."

"Can she have visitors?"

There was an audible sigh. "Chris, is Charles rubbing off on you?"

"What's that mean?" I said, knowing exactly what she meant.

"Are you going to start playing detective like your half-wit friend?"

"Of course not. Barb and I found her and so I wanted to see how she was doing."

"Yeah, right. To answer your innocent sounding question, yes, she can have visitors."

Cindy gave me the room number and a warning that if I started nosing in police business, she'd have me arrested for impersonating an officer, for gross stupidity, and for giving her ulcers. She hung up before I could thank her for being so kind to one of her constituents.

Chapter 4

Barb said she felt a connection to Joyce and offered to accompany me to the hospital. She also hinted that since we'd be in Charleston, it would be a great night to have supper at one of the city's many fine restaurants.

Joyce was barely recognizable as the person from the beach. Her hair that had been mixed with sand and in a state of disarray was now combed and while not styled, was passable. She looked to be in her forties and had healthy color in her cheeks as opposed to the white with a blue tinge they had on the beach. The look of confusion she gave us when we entered the room was replaced by a radiant smile of recognition.

"They tell me that you saved my life," she said, before we could speak. "Thank you."

Barb moved close to the bed and rested her hand on Joyce's shoulder. "We were worried about you. It's wonderful seeing you doing so well. I'm Barb and my friend is Chris."

I moved beside Barb and reached out and shook Joyce's hand. She let go and grabbed the television's remote and muted a game show that had an infuriatingly loud studio audience.

"Nice to meet you. Please have a seat."

There was only one chair, and I motioned for Barb to take it. I stood beside her and leaned on an over-bed table at the side of the room.

"I hope you don't mind us visiting," Barb said. "We were wondering how you were doing."

"Heavens, no. It's great seeing familiar faces. I wasn't at my best the last time I saw you."

"How are you feeling?" I asked.

"Fortunate. I have scrapes and bruises but nothing to complain about. They did an MRI on my brain, so I suppose I have one, although it's a bit scrambled. The main problem was hypothermia, and they had me drinking hot tea and wrapped in warm blankets. I'm fine now and told they're going to kick me out in the morning unless I take a turn for the worse."

I said, "Your name's Joyce?"

She lowered her gaze and in a faint voice said, "That's what they say."

"You don't remember?"

"No."

"It's none of our business," Barb said. "You don't have to tell us anything if you don't want. I was wondering what you remember."

"Like I told that lady police chief and a psychiatrist who visited me right before you got here, all I remember is being on a boat. Don't know where, what kind of boat, or who

24

else was on it. There was a storm and the next thing I remember was being in the water. Freezing water. I was holding on a surfboard for dear life. I remember seeing the words Ocean Pacific on the board. They said that's the brand. It's funny that I remember that. The next thing I knew was you leaning over me." She shook her head. "Barb, Chris, that's all, I mean all, I remember." She closed her eyes and whispered, "I didn't know my name was Joyce."

Barb said, "Was the psychiatrist helpful?"

"She was nice and listened. Helpful, I don't think so. She said I have amnesia, she called it a word I can't remember."

Barb said, "Retrograde."

I glanced at Barb and didn't say anything.

"That's it. Said it was caused by a trauma." She closed her eyes and Barb nodded toward the door.

"Joyce," I said, "we'd better let you get some rest. It's great seeing that you're doing so well."

Her eyes opened. "Thanks for coming. That was kind of you."

Barb and I patted her on the arm.

Joyce smiled up at us, and said, "What now?"

I wish we had an answer.

———

Barb was unusually quiet as I maneuvered through downtown Charleston on the way to Fleet Landing Restaurant and Bar, one of many nice restaurants in the city known for fine dining. Barb had never been there, but I'd been twice. The restaurant overlooked the Charleston Harbor and is near the Historic City Market with half of the eatery over water. Christmas lights decorated the entry and from our table we could see other seasonal lights from buildings along the waterfront.

Our server asked if we wanted drinks and an appetizer. We each ordered the house Cabernet while Barb scanned the menu. She added, "An order of Fleet Landing Stuffed Hush Puppies would be good."

Barb had the metabolism of a hummingbird and could out eat people twice her one-hundred-twenty pounds while never gaining an ounce. It was irritating. I had no idea what was stuffed in the hush puppies despite the menu saying it was a veloute of lobster, rock shrimp, and leeks. The server left, and I asked Barb what a veloute was.

"Clueless. Figured anything with hush puppies has to be good."

Her ignorance made me feel better, sort of. It was good hearing her speak after being unusually quiet since we'd left the hospital.

It was dark outside, and Barb nodded toward a row of lights from across the bay as they reflected on the calm water. "That's beautiful. I'm glad we came here."

I agreed, and in a lesson learned from Charles, she changed direction on a dime. "What do you think of her story?"

"I know little about amnesia. After Cal got hit on the head back in the summer he forgot recent events for a few days. The doc called it amnesia, but he could remember things from his past."

Cal Ballew was a friend who owned Cal's Country Bar and Burgers.

Barb said, "That was anterograde amnesia, where the person can't remember current information. His was caused by a brain trauma, the blow to the head. Joyce has retro-grade amnesia which is the opposite of anterograde. There are several other kinds of amnesia, but those are the two most common."

I nodded like I understood, which was partially true, and said, "You sure you didn't go to medical school rather than law school?"

She chuckled. "I had a client whose husband suffered from retrograde amnesia resulting from his mother's sudden death. The father died a few years earlier. There was a ton of money involved and my client had been told by her mother-in-law that the bulk of it was to go to her grandchil-dren and the humane society. The husband with amnesia said he couldn't remember but *knew* that wasn't true and that he was to inherit, and it was up to him to decide what to do with the estate. This is the kind of legal crap you step in when there's no will."

"They didn't have one?"

"No. My client's in-laws were in their fifties and thought they had plenty of time to worry about things like wills. Wrong. Anyway, I researched amnesia to represent her. One of the hardest things I did as an attorney was become an expert on oodles of things in which I had no interest."

"What happened with your client?"

"Other than me using my superior Penn State Law training to win a victory?"

"That goes without saying."

"Perhaps, but I like saying it. The other critical develop-ment was when my client's husband regained his memory and found a notarized letter he'd hidden that his mother had given him telling that he would get everything."

Thinking of Joyce, I said, "How long did it take for him to regain his memory?"

"Four months of legal wrestling and delaying depositions."

I smiled and turned serious. "Cal's amnesia was caused by the smack on the head. Joyce didn't have any apparent physical injury other than a few bruises and scrapes. What caused hers?"

"Most likely, a form of retrograde called psychological amnesia, also referred to as dissociative amnesia. It can be caused by a multitude of things, being the victim of a crime, child abuse, witnessing a traumatic event, on-and-on. Basically, any intolerable life situation that causes psychological stress can cause it. It's rare."

"Thank you, Doctor Barb. Any idea how long she could've had it?"

She smiled. "No. I missed that class in law school."

Our drinks arrived along with the appetizer. The server said the bar was backed up or we would've had our drinks sooner. Barb told her it wasn't a problem. Barb ordered shrimp and grits for her entrée. Grits were on my list of least favorite foods and I stuck with the chicken piccata. The server left, and Barb took a bite of the appetizer.

I thought about the causes of psychological amnesia, and said, "The first thing Joyce said she remembered was being on a boat, so wouldn't it make sense that whatever she suffered from occurred around that time?"

Barb held up a finger and pointed to her mouth. Talking with a mouthful of food wasn't unheard of among my friends. Barb had more class than most of them, so I waited.

She finished chewing, took a sip of water, and said, "Don't know."

I'd waited for that.

"Cal's doctor said that time was the best cure for his amnesia. It was a week before he regained most of his memory. It was scrambled at first, but finally returned to his pre-traumatic head bashing. What treatments are there to help Joyce?"

"Time is the best. If there are underlying physical or mental disorders, psychotherapy could help. Family support is also critical. Orientation aids such as photos, familiar smells, and even music can speed up remembering the past."

"That's if the police find her family."

"That could be awhile unless someone reports her missing. She could be from anywhere." Barb turned to the large windows that overlooked the harbor. "Look how beautiful the flickering Christmas lights look on the surface of the water."

That was her way of saying we'd talked enough about Joyce. We spent the next hour enjoying the scenery, each other's company, and a wonderful meal. She told me about Troy and Nate, two men from Canada, who'd rented the condo next to her for a month and how much they were enjoying the "balmy" December weather on Folly. She crossed her arms and made a shivering motion as she said it.

Several units in Barb's condo complex were vacation rentals, and she never knew from week to week who some of her neighbors would be. That would bother me, but she said it was interesting seeing who was staying there, and besides, the high turnover meant more books she'd sell in her store.

The ride to Folly was peaceful and quiet, and I couldn't help smiling at the brightly lit crab, dolphin, turtle, and sand dollar decorations that adorned light poles at each intersection along Center Street. I also couldn't stop thinking about the first or last name woman named Joyce. And, that she was going to be released tomorrow. Released to go where?

Chapter 5

I sat up in bed and wondered why I hadn't thought of it earlier. I'd slept later than usual, and the low December sun filtered through the blinds. Was it too early to call Chief LaMond? Over the years, I'd called her several times before eight o'clock and she'd berated me for pestering her before her work day began. I smiled, picked up the phone, and recalled that she'd also berated me for calling during work hours, after her work day, and on weekends and holidays.

"What in the Elf on the Shelf are you pestering me about before I've had time to enjoy a hot brew of hazelnut coffee with my adorable hubby?"

"Elf on the Shelf?"

"You know, Santa's danged scout elf that parents use to trick their kids into being nice rather than naughty before Christmas. Hate that thing, hate ads for it, hate seeing it sneaking around the house."

I was vaguely aware of the Elf, but never considered it a four-letter word. "Did Larry put one in your house?"

I didn't think she was going to answer. She finally said, "If I hear one word about it from anyone other than you, you will not live long enough to get a lump of coal from Santa. Now, in case your feeble mind forgot, you called me. Would it be rude to ask why?"

After the Elf talk, I'd almost forgotten the reason. I stifled a chuckle, and said, "Any word on who Joyce is, or what happened to her?"

"Double no."

"That's what I was afraid of. Barb and I stopped by the hospital to see her. She was doing well and said they might release her today. Where will she go?"

"For being such an infuriating pest, you occasionally come up with a good question. That's one of them. My answer is one I give more and more. I don't have a freakin' clue. The hospital has a case worker who'll work with her. Joyce isn't in medical distress, so the options are limited."

"What if I have a possible solution?"

"Hence the reason for this ungodly early call?"

"An astute observation, Chief LaMond."

"Any chance you would share it?"

"Yes." And I did.

She said my idea wasn't horrible, which I took to mean she thought it was great. She asked me to let her know the results. I said I would, and she asked if she could get back to her coffee and peaceful morning. I said yes, and she hung up before I could add anything to spoil it.

My next call was to Preacher Burl Costello who answered in a better mood than had Cindy. I asked if it was too early to call and he laughed and said no that his residents were up and clanking around all hours of day and night. I asked if he was entertaining visitors and he said he was if I was the visitor.

Fifteen minutes later, I pulled in the gravel parking area in front of the large, wood-frame house. A massive live oak butted up to the house on one side and smaller trees and shrubs were grouped on two other sides. The structure was at least fifty years old and its north-facing wall was covered with moss. Despite its unkept appearance, the house had weathered many a storm and was sturdier than most of the houses surrounding it. White, LED Christmas lights were strung around the door frame and along the roofline.

The front door was open and a man in his mid-thirties and cut-off jeans despite the temperature in the forties was on his knees and working on the lock. I asked if the preacher was available and he said for me to go in and yell.

I stepped in the narrow hallway and didn't have to yell. Preacher Burl saw me, shook my hand, said he was waiting for me, and asked if I wanted coffee. Chief LaMond could learn hospitality skills from the preacher. He led me through a long, center hallway. The wallcovering reminded me of a rainforest with its various shades of green and a dark over-cast feel. It was ripped in a couple of spots and gave a depressing feel to the house. At the end of the hall, Burl turned left, and I followed him to the large kitchen, the kind in country farmhouses.

A woman was taking something out of the stove and was startled by our entry. "Sorry, Sister Adrienne," Burl said, "Meet my friend, Brother Chris. Brother Chris, Sister Adrienne was the first person to move in when Hope House opened. She's a great cook and we're fortunate to have her."

Adrienne was probably in her fifties, paper thin and wore her graying black hair in a bun. I told her it was nice meeting her, and she said likewise although I didn't detect a great deal of sincerity. Burl poured two cups of coffee while I was having my awkward conversation with Adrienne, and suggested I follow him to the living room.

"Adrienne's not great with people, especially men," Burl said, as he pointed to the brown vinyl-covered sofa with chrome legs that'd look at home in a doctor's waiting room. He lowered his voice. "Her husband left her for his massage therapist. Poor Adrienne took solace in alcohol before finding the Lord and First Light Church. She now works for a landscaper and by the grace of God, will be moving to an apartment all her own come summer. The move will be wonderful for her, bad for our quality of meals." Burl patted his stomach.

The waiting-room-style sofa was out of place in a residence, but various Christmas decorations warmed the room. A seven-foot-tall pine tree stood in the corner and was wrapped with colorful lights, and adorned with silver and gold ornaments, plus a few homemade, cardboard decorations. A dozen or so colorfully wrapped packages rested on the tree skirt. I smiled at how cheerful the room was. Burl took a sip from his mug and leaned back on the sofa. Adrienne's story was interesting, but time was important, so I wanted to share the reason for my visit.

"Preacher, the other day when you were in the Dog, you said you had four residents and six bedrooms. Has the number of residents increased since then?"

"No. The house was not created to be a permanent home for its residents. Since I've opened, we've had several come and go. In addition to Adrienne, we have Taylor Strong, the gentleman working on the broken lock on the front door, Rebekah Leachmen, she's at work at Black

34

Magic Cafe, been there going on six months and doing well. You just missed her. Then there's Bernard Prine. You're the reason Brother Bernard is here."

I'd met Bernard a year ago. He was homeless, and I learned he'd been a war hero, had received a serious head injury in Afghanistan, and suffered from PTSD, or PTSS as it's now called. He'd been kicked out of several homeless shelters because of his temper and when I told him about Preacher Burl, Bernard sought him out and the two were good for each other. I thanked Burl for all he'd done for Bernard.

"Brother Chris, I don't suppose you're here to take an inventory of my residents."

I told him no, and that I was there to see if he could provide lodging for Joyce.

He said that it would be his Christian duty, and that, "It would be a joy to do so. In fact, if acceptable with her, I will call her Joy." He made an exaggerated nod. "'Tis the season of tidings of comfort and joy."

She didn't remember her name was Joyce, so I told him I doubted she'd mind him calling her the shortened version. I also said I didn't know if the hospital would release her to him. He smiled and said one of his flock, which is what he called members of First Light, had been in the hospital, and he got to know someone in the discharge department, and would call her. After he brings Joy to Hope House, he said he'd contact Chief LaMond and tell her, so she would know where to reach Joy if her identity was discovered. I appreciated that he was willing to take charge of these tasks and asked that he let me know what happens. I also told him how admirable I thought it was for him to have opened the house and asked if it was too much for him to shoulder alone.

He laughed. "I've thought that several times a day. Sister Lottie volunteers when I need extra help, which is often. As I shared with you when we first met, I have carpentry skills and they're being utilized more than I ever imagined. Three of the windows leaked when it rained, and there are more holes in the drywall than I can count. One of my previous residents was a finish carpenter and a tremendous help, a gift from heaven, you might say. I was happy for him and saddened for Hope House when he was offered a high-paying job in Summerville and was able to afford an apartment. It was a sad day indeed when he left. Regardless, Lottie does the best she can, and is especially good with the women."

Lottie was the first member of First Light and after some of us had pestered Burl about it, he realized that she wanted more than a preacher/member relationship. They've dated several months and the rumor among members of the flock was that they might soon be seeking another preacher. More specifically, a preacher to perform their wedding ceremony. I hoped it was true.

"That's good." I looked out the window. "Any static from neighbors about this type of establishment in the neighborhood?"

"Some looked askance at first, but I have strict rules and any violation is cause for immediate removal. Most of the folks who end up here are temporarily, shall I say, disenfranchised, and find their way back to a productive member of society. Or, they have been to this point."

"Preacher, there's one other thing I should mention. All

that Joyce, Joy, remembers is being on a boat and then in the ocean clinging to a surfboard, before Barb and I found her."

"I was aware of that, Brother Chris."

"Then you know it's possible something happened on the boat that could've caused her amnesia. Something bad. Whoever was on the boat may not know that she survived. Or, if they do, they may try something."

Burl nodded. "In other words, the fewer people who know she's here the better."

"It'd be best if no one knew."

"My guests will know, and I feel I must tell Lottie since she's good with the women."

"That's fine. If we can keep it to those few along with the police, it'd be best."

Our conversation ended with a sales pitch from Preacher Burl for me to attend his Sunday service and his special Christmas Eve service. I told him I'd try. He didn't appear convinced. Neither did I.

Chapter 6

I hadn't told Charles what I'd learned from Cindy, or from the visit to the hospital. I called, and he suggested that our conversation would best take place over an early lunch at the Crab Shack. The popular restaurant was halfway between Charles's apartment on Sandbar Lane and my cottage on East Ashley Avenue. The temperature was still in the forties, yet I decided to walk. The exercise would do me good.

"About time you got here," Charles said, as he grabbed a peanut out of the cardboard container in front of him. He wore a red and blue Walters State long-sleeve sweatshirt, and jeans. My friend has one of the largest collections of college and university logoed sweatshirts this side of Dick's Sporting Goods. I'd tried to find out why he has them and where they came from. The best answer he'd come up with was, "Here and there." I stopped asking years ago, although it never stopped him from sharing trivia about the shirts.

He pointed to his chest. "I know you're wondering,

they're the Senators. It's in Morristown, Tennessee."

See?

"Good morning, Charles," I said, ignoring his comment about me being late and the college highlighted on his torso. I picked a nut out of the container and cracked it open.

He sighed. My disinterest annoyed him, but I knew what I was going to share next would hold his attention.

"Barb and I visited Joyce in the hospital. She—"

He grabbed another nut and pointed it at me. "Who's Joyce?"

I realized I hadn't told him about yesterday's conversation with Cindy.

"Chief LaMond found the name in the sweatshirt of the woman Barb and I found on the beach."

His eyes narrowed. "When did you talk to Cindy?"

"Late yesterday," I said, a slight time-shift.

"You didn't call to tell me like you said you would, and then you called Barb and invited her instead of me to visit Jane Doe, umm, Joyce, in the hospital. Oh, and then you got home and instead of calling me, you did whatever you did at home. How am I doing?"

"Time got away."

And, I haven't even mentioned meeting with Preacher Burl and what's going to happen next. Before I could dig a deeper hole, Kaylee, the server, appeared and asked if we were ready to order. She glanced at the container of peanuts and added, "Something other than freebees."

We took the hint and ordered flounder crunch sandwiches and refills on the water she'd added to our table while we were gorging on peanuts.

Kaylee's timely interruption took the steam out of Charles's rant.

He leaned back, slowly shook his head, and said, "You went to the hospital without me?"

I thought that was self-evident but understood where he was going. "Yes. I thought about asking if you wanted to go but figured Joyce wouldn't be comfortable with two strange guys visiting."

"Barb and I could've visited while you stayed in the car. After all, I'm the detective. I could've found out…never mind, what'd you learn?"

"Nothing more than I told you the last time we talked. She has retrograde amnesia and doesn't remember anything before being on a boat, and even then, she doesn't remember what happened."

"That's horrible. When will she be well enough to get out of the hospital?"

"Could be today."

Charles leaned his elbows on the table and stared at me. "Where's she going? If she can't remember anything, what'll happen to her?"

I tightened my grip on the plastic water glass and prepared for rant number two. "Preacher Burl said he would see if he could get her released to Hope House. If he can, then—"

Charles leaned across the table and waved his hand in my face. "Whoa. When did this happen? How do you know?"

"That's why I called you as soon as I left Burl," I said, emphasis on *as soon as*.

Food arrived along with more questions. "When's her memory coming back? Will Burl be able to take her to Hope House? Do you think she's still in danger?" He hesitated and took a bite of his sandwich, and then with food in his mouth, said, "How're we going to find out who she is and what happened?"

Instead of saying, "I don't know?" four times, I shrugged and stuck a fry in my mouth.

I was seated facing a colorful mural featuring the Ferris wheel that once towered over Folly and Charles was facing the entry. He jumped up and headed toward the door. I turned to see what'd grabbed his attention and saw Chief LaMond talking to the hostess. Charles joined them and pointed at our table. I imagined that Cindy was thinking she'd chosen the wrong restaurant for lunch. I smiled as Charles put his arm around her shoulder and escorted her to the table and pulled out the chair beside his and motioned for her to join us.

"Hey, Chris, look who wanted to sit with us."

Wanted to turn and run out the door as soon as she saw Charles, would've been my guess. "Glad you could join us."

She glared at me like it was my fault she chose the wrong restaurant for a peaceful meal.

Charles pretended not to see Cindy's glare, and said, "We were talking about the lady Chris and Barb found surfing. He was getting ready to call you and see if you learned who she is and what happened." Charles turned to me.

Cindy glanced at me. "Hmm, is that right?"

"Have you found out who she is?" I asked, skirting Charles's claim that I was going to call.

Kaylee returned to the table and asked Cindy what she wanted for lunch.

"I'd like three bourbons and a liter of gin to put up with these troublemakers. Instead, how about water and whatever they're having."

Cindy shook her head as Kaylee headed to the kitchen.

"No, I don't know who she is. There are no missing person reports fitting her description, and her prints aren't in the system. She's still Joyce Doe or Jane Joyce, depending on if Joyce is her first or last name."

I was tempted to tell her that Burl had shortened it to Joy. Instead, I told her of my conversation with Burl and that he was contacting the hospital to see if she could stay at Hope House. Rather than Cindy getting mad at me, and I suppose Burl, for butting in, she said she was glad. She'd be closer when her memory starts returning.

Her food arrived. I'd observed over the years how much quicker a police chief gets served than other mortals. Cindy took a sip of water and a bite of sandwich.

Charles took the break in her talking to ask, "Learn anything else?"

Cindy looked at Charles and rolled her eyes. "Yep, two things."

"Well?" Charles said.

"First, to case the inside of a restaurant before coming in. Peace, quiet, and a relaxing lunch don't go with Chris, Charles, and your pestering."

"Second?" Charles said.

"Do you know Jamison and Renee Caulder?"

I said, "Don't think so."

"I know Renee." Charles said. "Met her walking her dog Bowser. Adorable Pekingese pup, originally from China, Pekingese dogs, not Renee. They're also called lion dogs because they look like the Chinese guardian lions that—"

"Enough," Cindy interrupted.

I silently seconded that.

She continued, "The Caulders are a nice couple. Jamison retired early from a highfalutin, high-paying job, and bought a house out on Tabby Drive that backs up to the river and the marsh. They've got a walking pier that goes from their deck to the river. The last few days they've been up in Asheville visiting relatives and spending some of their oodles of dollars. They got home late yesterday and guess what was missing from their nice little walking pier?"

I didn't know, but knew it was interesting or Cindy wouldn't be telling the story. "What?"

"Their cute little eighteen-foot Tahoe Q4i runabout."

"Do they know when the boat was taken?" I asked.

"Nope, and neither did their neighbors. The people in the nearest house were in Phoenix until yesterday. They're the ones who noticed it missing and told Jamison when he got home."

"Don't suppose anyone's found a lost eighteen-foot-long boat?" Charles said.

Cindy smiled. "Finally, a question I can answer. Yep."

"Someone found it?" I asked.

She nodded. "Not far from where it was taken. It was tied to a pier, a piss-poor knot, I might add. It was behind a deserted house on Seacrest Lane. Some guy a couple of houses away saw it and didn't think anything of it until his wife who likes to stick her nose in everyone's business—like you, Charles—said it didn't belong there and made him call us."

I said, "I don't suppose you found any prints on it."

"Only Jamison and Renee's. Also found an ignition that'd been mangled and hotwired. Want to guess what we didn't find?"

"Not Bowser, I hope," Charles said.

Cindy sighed, and said, "He went with them to Asheville."

"What didn't you find?" I asked.

"Jamison's surfboard."

"Let me guess," I said. "Ocean Pacific?"

Cindy smiled. "You win the opportunity to pay for my lunch."

"Chris always wins the good stuff," Charles said, through smiling teeth.

I ignored him. "So, you think someone hotwired the boat, somehow and somewhere got Joyce on board, and took her out in the ocean to what?"

"A theory is that it was to get her far enough off shore to throw her overboard. Mind you, that's mere speculation. Until her memory returns, we don't know anything other than the boat was stolen."

"What about the surfboard?" Charles asked.

"Charles, did you miss the part where I said, way back thirty seconds ago, that all we know is that the boat was stolen?"

Charles stuffed a fry in his mouth, nodded twice, and said, "So, Chief, what do you want us to do to help figure out what happened out on the deep-blue sea?"

She looked up from her plate, glared at Charles, and said, "In the spirit of the big guy in the red suit coming next week to visit all little chillins, and big chillins like you, Charles, I say Ho, Ho, Ho! In case that's not clear, it means I'm laughing at your suggestion and the best way you can help is to stay out of our way. Leave the coppin' to cops."

Charles took the hint, or decided it wasn't time to argue, and said, "That's a good idea, Chief."

I'd known Charles for a long time, knew his moods, knew his approach to most everything. I also knew he was lying through his teeth.

Chapter 7

There was a good chance that Joyce had been on the stolen boat, yet several questions remained. Those questions kept me awake most of the night. Who was Joyce, be it her first or last name? What trauma erased her past? Will her memory return? If she's from the area, why hadn't someone reported her missing? And, if she'd been on the stolen boat, why?

I must have fallen asleep at some point. The phone jarred me awake at seven-thirty.

"Brother Chris, did I awaken you?"

I lied and said, no.

"Good. I was excited and wanted you to be first to know. I have been given authorization to collect Joy and bring her here. Praise the Lord."

"That's great news, Preacher. Do you know when she'll be released?"

"They said I could come over now, and they'll discharge her when I get there."

"Great," I repeated.

"Brother Chris, might I ask a huge favor?"

"Sure."

"Would you go with me? You're a familiar face to her. I know she'd appreciate you being there."

"I'd be glad to."

Burl's granite-gray Dodge Grand Caravan pulled in the drive fifteen minutes after I'd agreed to go, and thirty minutes later we were in the hospital visitor's lot.

Burl stepped behind me as I approached Joyce's door, and said, "Since she knows you, why don't you go in first?"

The patient was sitting on the chair. Her hair was pulled in a ponytail and she wore a long-sleeve, blue T-shirt and the same slacks she had on when we found her. Someone must've given her the shirt and had the slacks cleaned since they were sand free and pressed. She smiled when I entered. The smile lessened when she saw the man behind me.

"You look great," I said. "Ready to get out of here?"

"Yes, but I don't have anywhere—"

"Good morning, Sister Joy, I'm Preacher Burl Costello."

Joyce glanced at Burl and quickly turned to me. "Chris, what's going on?"

I smiled and hoped it put her at ease. "Joyce, Preacher Burl is a friend and the minister of First Light Church on Folly Beach. Part of First Light's ministry is a large house where several people live. Preacher Burl talked to one of the hospital administrators and he agreed to let you stay there until you can get on your feet and your memory returns."

"But, I don't have money. I can't afford—"

Burl took a step closer to Joyce and said, "Sister Joy—"

"Sir, who's Joy, and what's this sister stuff? I'm not your sister… I don't think."

"Joyce," I said, "Preacher Burl calls those who attend First Light either brother or sister. Your name's Joyce, so he thought Joy was a pretty sounding name."

Burl added, "Christmas is right around the corner, so I thought calling you that would be reflective of the joy you will bring to us all."

"Preacher, no offense. I don't know you, crap, pardon my language, I don't even know me. What makes you think I'll bring joy? For all you know, for all I know, I could be a serial killer, or I don't know what."

I wondered the same thing and waited for Burl's response.

He rubbed his hand through his bristle-brush mustache. "Joyce, I hope you don't mind me calling you Joy. As you can tell from looking at this rough-hewn face, I've been around the block a time or two. I've seen evil up close. Regardless, I believe the good in people. Yes, there's a chance that you might not be a saint." He chuckled. "The Good Lord knows I'm not. I see a lady who's suffered a terrible fate. I can't imagine how horrific it must be to not remember the past. I see a lady who needs a break or two to get back on her feet. And, I see someone I, even with my meager resources, can provide a comfortable bed, decent meals, and others who can share with you their hopes and dreams. I would be honored to have you as a part of Hope House for as long as you need, or want, to be there."

She gave a faint smile and said in a faint voice so that Burl and I had to lean closer to hear, "That's kind of you, sir, but I don't have money. I can't afford to pay."

"Ah, Sister Joy, you're in luck. You qualify for the special close-to-Christmas rent of zero dollars a week. And, for no additional charge, Chris and I will provide transportation to your new home."

"Are you certain, Burl, umm, Preacher?"

"Absolutely."

She gave Burl a tentative hug, and whispered, "Thank you."

I gave a sigh of relief.

After what seemed like an eternity getting Joy discharged, the ride to Folly was awkward at best. Burl tried to explain how he founded First Light two years ago and how it met most Sundays on the beach near the Folly Beach Fishing Pier, and during inclement weather, in a storefront on Center Street next to Barb's Books. I shared how I met the preacher when my photo gallery occupied the space where Barb's is now. I didn't get into the deaths that surrounded First Light's first few months in existence.

Joy alternated between listening to Burl patter on about First Light and staring out the window with her mind wandering. Burl didn't notice the difference until he asked if she would be interested in attending his Sunday service in two days.

"I'm sorry, Preacher. What?"

He repeated the question.

"Preacher, are there other churches on Folly?"

"Excellent question, Sister Joy. There are three other wonderful houses of worship on our tiny island. The Baptist, Catholic, and Methodist churches are within sight of each other."

She turned from staring out the window to Burl. "Why start another one?"

"Another excellent question, my dear. First Light is nondenominational and attracts men and women who, for whatever reason, are not attracted to the more traditional denominations." He laughed. "Some of the first to attend were surfers who'd been on the beach waiting to ply their skill in the waves. I'd love to say that my wonderful, spiritual, and inspirational message drew them in. They finally told me that they were bored waiting for, as they said, 'boss' waves, and enjoyed the group singing."

Joy said, "That must've been disheartening."

Burl patted her on the arm. "To the contrary. As I often share from the pulpit, God works in strange and mysterious ways. That day, He provided a flat sea to prevent the young people from surfing and provided members of the flock singing at the top of their lungs to attract those nearby. Several of the surfers have attended religiously, pun intended, since that glorious day."

Burl pulled in my drive and I said it was nice seeing Joy again and that she would find Hope House and Preacher Burl to her liking. I had no idea if that was true, but wanted to reinforce the decision for her to stay there. In a less than convincing tone, she said she hoped so. Our conversation ended with her thanking me for coming with Burl to pick her up and for me to say hi to Barb.

The first thing I did when I got in the house was call Charles to let him know the latest on Joy. I was pleased when he didn't scold me for waiting to tell him. He added that he was planning to attend First Light's next service. I said I might see him there, emphasis on might. I was an irregular attender which meant I attended more often than Christmas and Easter, but less, far less, than weekly.

Charles thought he had my commitment to attend, then asked if Joy had regained her memory and shared with me what had happened on the boat.

"Charles, don't you think if that happened, I would've led with it?"

"Does that mean she doesn't remember?"

"No more than the last time we talked."

"Doesn't give us much to work with finding out what happened, does it?"

"We're not trying to find out, remember?"

"Good Ole Abe Lincoln said, 'How many legs does a dog have if you call the tail a leg? Calling a tail a leg doesn't make it a leg.'"

Another of Charles's quirks was quoting United States Presidents, or he said they were actual quotes. I had never taken the time to research their origin. As Chris Landrum said, I don't care an atom if they are. That sentiment was shared by others who knew my friend, although it didn't stop him from spewing them.

"Your point is?"

"The point, my friend, is whether you say you are or not, you along with the help of your trusty sidekick are on the case. You can deny it to Cindy, to Burl, to anyone who will listen, and to the Caulders' dog Bowser. That still don't mean you ain't trying."

"Whatever."

He laughed, and the phone went dead.

Chapter 8

Moving to a strange house, surrounded by strangers, and not knowing who you are, where you came from, or anything about your past, had to be traumatic. I decided to drop by and see how Joy was adjusting. I didn't have anything encouraging to offer except a face that she'd known longer than anyone there. I hoped that would be enough.

It took three knocks before Bernard Prine opened the door. I hardly recognized him. When we'd met a year ago, he had stringy, dark-brown hair, a week-old beard, and wore a faded army jacket and gray dress slacks two sizes too large. Now, his hair was neatly trimmed and combed, he had on a long-sleeve, yellow dress shirt, black jeans, new tennis shoes, and a smile he'd seldom shared a year ago.

"Well if it isn't my friend, Chris Landrum," Bernard said in a Southern drawl. "Welcome, sir."

We'd had little contact since last Christmas, so I was pleased that he'd referred to me as a friend. He shook my hand with a grip powerful enough to open a stubborn food jar.

"It's good to see you, Bernard. How do you like it here?"

He smiled. "One of the best things that ever happened to me was last Christmas when you told me that I could talk to Preacher Burl about my issues. He's a godsend. Crap— whoops, Preacher doesn't like me saying crap—umm, phooey, even if he wasn't a preacher, I'd still say he's a godsend. He's provided room and board, lent me a few dollars when I've needed them, and best of all, he's been there when I sort of threw a couple of temper tantrums, the kind that got me kicked out of homeless shelters. Preacher put his arm around me and took me aside and talked me through whatever inspired me to make an ass, umm, a fool out of myself. I'd do anything for that man."

"I'm glad to hear it. Is your newest resident around?"

"Yes, sir. We were in the kitchen having coffee with Preacher Burl. How about joining us?"

He was leading me to the kitchen before I could answer. We passed one of the female residents, Adrienne, I believe. She was dressed in a light jacket, jeans that were no stranger to manual labor, and calf-high, leather work boots.

Bernard said, "Off to work?"

Adrienne lowered her eyes when she saw me, and mumbled, "Yes."

She headed to the door, and Bernard leaned close and whispered, "If you ask me, she's housing a herd of secrets."

Coming from Bernard, that was something. I remembered how many times Charles and I tried to get him to tell us where he was living when we first met. He never would.

"What kind of secrets?"

He rubbed his chin and stared as Adrienne exited. "If I

knew, they wouldn't be secrets. Reckon it's a feeling I get when I'm around her." He shrugged.

Burl was pouring coffee in a mug in front of Joy, and she was laughing.

He saw me in the doorway and without skipping a beat, grabbed another mug, filled it, and handed it to me.

"Brother Chris, if you'd arrived a half hour earlier, you could have joined us for breakfast."

"Yes," Bernard said, "we had crepes, blackberry-mint scones, arugula and pistachio pesto quiche, and, oh yeah, crumpets."

"Really?" I said.

Burl laughed, and said, "Brother Chris, we had a bowl of Raisin Bran and orange juice."

I had forgotten Bernard's sense of humor. "Sounds good."

Bernard glanced at Burl and said, "I must've been thinking about yesterday."

Joy ignored the factual and fictional breakfast menu, and said, "Chris, it's nice to see you again."

"You too, Joy. How do you like it here?"

"It's far better than the room at the hospital. Preacher Burl gave me a choice of two bedrooms and I picked the one with two windows instead of one."

"Brother Taylor moved out and looks like Sister Rebekah will be leaving soon. She's doing well at her job at Black Magic and will be moving to her own apartment after Christmas."

"It's great that your residents find places to live," I said.

"They're blessed, yet I'm always sad to see them go."

Bernard pointed his mug at Burl. "Don't worry, Preacher. I won't leave you."

Burl chuckled. "You have a home here as long as you wish."

Bernard took the last sip and excused himself saying that he thought a walk would do him good. He headed out the back door, and I told him it was good seeing him again.

Joy whispered something I couldn't understand. Apparently, Burl couldn't either and asked her to repeat it.

She stared in her mug and said, "What if I have a house somewhere? What if I have a husband, children? Brothers, sisters, parents? What if…" She held out her hands palms up and repeated, "What if?"

Burl reached out and hugged her. I didn't know what to say and sipped coffee.

A minute later, Joy stepped back from Burl and said, "If you gentlemen don't mind, I'd like to go to my room."

Burl said, "Joy, this is now your home. Feel free to come, go, and do as you please. I lock the doors each night, but I'll give you a key. And, I'm here if you need anything."

She nodded and left the kitchen.

Burl watched her go, and said, "Christmas is a week away and the best gift in the world for Sister Joy would be her memory. I can't give that to her."

"None of us can. What you are giving are some of the greatest gifts possible, a place to call home and a loving environment."

"Yes," Burl said, "I'm afraid that isn't enough when it comes to Sister Joy. My other residents know where they've been yet are uncertain of their future. That's why most end up under this roof. Without knowledge of her past, Sister Joy can't determine whether staying here is a good or a bad thing. She has no perspective on her reality."

"Did she share anything beyond being on the boat?"

He shook his head. "Nothing like a direct memory, but here's something. I was showing her around upstairs and she pointed to a couple of places where I needed to repair the wood trim. She said she could help."

"Perhaps she has construction experience."

"Maybe, although not necessarily," Burl said. "I told her I'd worked construction back in the day. She could've wanted to help and figured I'd show her what to do. She wants to help."

"True. Did she say anything else?"

"No."

"What did you tell the others about her?"

"Nothing other than she's been in the hospital and would be staying here until she got back on her feet."

"Did you say anything about her memory?"

"I told them that she was foggy about the past."

"How does she get along with them?"

"There's been little contact. She stayed in her room most of time. She talked for a while to Bernard, but little to the others."

"Preacher, I'm still worried that there is someone who may want to harm her. Have you told everyone that it's important that they don't talk about her with anyone outside this house?"

"I told Sister Adrienne and Brother Bernard. I haven't had a chance to talk with Rebekah. I will when she returns from work. More coffee?"

I told him I was okay, and he said, "Now, a question. Have the police learned anything about what happened?"

I told him about the stolen boat and surfboard.

"They're certain that the surfboard was the same one you and Sister Barb found with Joy?"

I nodded.

"Have they checked the boat for fingerprints?"

"Chief LaMond said there weren't any except those of the owners."

I told him I'd better be going and asked him to call if Joy said anything that would help the police.

He said he would and ended with, "I look forward to seeing you at tomorrow's worship service."

How could I say no to that?

Chapter 9

A clear, pollution-free sky greeted me as I left the house to walk to the morning service at First Light. The temperature was flirting with the upper thirties, so I headed three blocks to the church's inclement weather sanctuary. Attendance was lower when the service was indoors, and approximately twenty people were standing around a coffee pot in back of the room. It was easy to spot Preacher Burl. He was wearing a white robe crafted from a bedsheet and pouring coffee in a Styrofoam cup. Lottie was nearby. I was reminded of the first time I'd seen her. She was in this building and helping Burl and a few others refinish discarded church pews to use in the sanctuary. She wore oversized clothes hiding her attractive figure and had a self-cut hairstyle. Today she looked and acted the part of a preacher's wife, something I hoped she'd soon become. She handed coffee to William Hansel, another friend of mine and a regular at First Light.

Joy was in the corner in animated conversation with Bernard. She had on a tan blouse and dress slacks, clothes I assumed donated by one of the other residents. It was good seeing her socializing. Amber and Jason, her nineteen-year-old son, were in the front of the room talking to a woman I didn't know.

Charles was huddled with Mary Ewing and her girls, Jewel, seven, and Joanie, three. Mary had been homeless until Preacher Burl learned of her plight a year ago and worked with her to find a house to share with two women, and to get a job at Bert's Market. Charles saw me, glanced at his bare wrist, and shook his head like he was scolding me for being late.

I was on my way to talk to Charles, Mary, Joanie and Jewel, when Lottie whispered something to Burl and he moved to an old lectern that'd spent its better years in a high school gymnasium. The preacher cleared his throat, and said, "Please repose thy selves." He pointed to the pews.

A couple of older ladies I didn't know moved to the front row and reposed thy selves. They were followed by three more members who heeded his charge. The others either weren't ready to stop socializing or didn't know what the preacher meant. I knew because he announced the beginning of many services with those words, so the regulars who hadn't moved, weren't ready to.

Burl tapped his hand on the lectern and repeated his "call to worship," and gained the attention of the remaining talkers. Dude Sloan was among that group. He'd seldom attended First Light until earlier this year when one of his employees was killed attempting to save Barb from the hands of a man trying to kill her.

I was going to see if Joy wanted to sit with me, but she was already seated beside Bernard. I slid in the pew next to Dude as Preacher Burl was saying something that began each service. "Please silence thy portable communication devices." Most did, and Burl asked William Hansel to lead the group in singing "Away in a Manger" from the songbook made from sheets of paper stapled together. The songs had been photocopied from a church hymnal.

William had a phenomenal voice and most of us, including me, knew that unless we could improve on the song, we shouldn't try. We mouthed the words as we listened to him sing. Burl's flock was kind, considerate, and many other good things, but except for William, singers we were not.

Burl was in his element, standing in front of *his flock*, sharing a lesson from the Gospel, and reminding us of the historic and spiritual events leading to Christmas, seven days away. Joy was staring at the preacher, and I wondered what was going through her mind.

Burl announced two services for next weekend. He called the first a Christmas Eve midnight service while at the same time saying it'd begin at seven o'clock. He joked—I assume he was joking—that it would be held then instead of midnight because his message would be more meaningful if his flock was sober, and there was a better chance of that at seven. He then said the Christmas morning service would be at the regular eleven o'clock time. Today's service concluded with William singing "O Come All Ye Faithful" with a few of us humming along and the rest mouthing the words.

Charles was on the sidewalk talking to the two women who'd been on the front pew. I stood aside until he patted each of them on the back and they walked away.

"Who're they? I don't remember seeing them before."

Charles watched the ladies go, and said, "You have to come to the service to see who's here."

Touché. "So, who are they?"

"Dixie and Martha."

"Dixie?"

"Doubt it says that on her birth certificate. That's all I've ever heard her called. She lives in the three hundred block of East Arctic across the street from Martha. Dixie's an ubergardener."

"A what?"

"A super-duper gardener. Her back yard is full of plants, flowers, herbs, and other growing things. Rumor is she has name holders beside each plant with the name, both the common name and the Latin name, printed on them."

"Why?"

Charles rolled his eyes. "Why do you wear boring clothes instead of educational, inspirational, and nifty shirts like *moi*?"

"What's that have to do with Dixie posting names of each of her…plant things?"

"Same answer to each question. Because she wants to."

"That helps."

He rolled his eyes, again. "Can I get back to what I was saying?"

"Please do."

"Martha and Dixie are widows. Kind of quiet, don't think they get out much. I occasionally see Martha walking around carrying a cane." He waved his handmade wooden cane in the air. "Not nice like this, one of those silver ones they sell at Harris Teeter. Enough about them, learn anything new about Joy?"

I told him no, and he was interrupted from asking me why not when Burl approached and said that he, Lottie, Joy, Bernard, and Dude were heading to Loggerhead's for lunch, and wondered if we would like to join them. The invitation was kind, participation by Dude unusual, and the chance for Charles to grill Joy about her past impossible to turn down. He answered yes for both of us.

Loggerhead's was on West Arctic Avenue, four blocks from First Light's foul-weather sanctuary, and across the street from Barb's condo in the Oceanfront Villas. Burl had removed his robe/sheet, so he didn't look like a ghost as we followed him to the restaurant. Charles spent the entire walk talking to Joy, not surprising knowing how curious—nosy— he was. In better weather, the large outside bar and dining area would have been packed. Today we were forced to move inside. Burl must have used his heavenly influence since there was a table available large enough to accommodate our group.

Yvonne, one of the owners, greeted us and said that Joe would be taking care of us. Joe, a long-tenured employee I'd known for a few years, was close behind Yvonne and took our drink orders. Five of us said water would be fine while Burl and Lottie ordered Diet Pepsi.

We were seated at a large, bar-height, rectangular table with Burl at the head and three of us seated on each of its long sides. Various NFL games were on televisions strategically located throughout the room.

"Thank you for breaking bread with me this lovely sabbath," Burl said, sounding more like a prayer than something you would normally hear in a bar.

Lottie was closest to Burl and patted him on the arm. "Preacher, we're delighted to join you."

Joy and Dude were seated next to Lottie and across from Bernard, Charles, and me. Bernard spoke next, but it was so loud in the room that I couldn't hear what he was saying.

Joy and Burl laughed, so it must've been humorous. It was good seeing Joy fitting in.

Our drinks arrived, and Dude stood, raised his glass and said, "Toast. Boss preacher."

Dude wore one of his many tie-dyed shirts, was in his mid-sixties and looked like the stereotype of an aging hippie, which he happened to be. He also had a way with words, a way to mangle them.

The rest of us raised our glasses to toast while Joy looked at the lifelong surfer like he was speaking Tigrinya. I told Joy that Dude owned the surf shop and had been on Folly many years. I failed to mention that despite his appearance, and extensive vocabulary that may exceed fifty words, that he was one of the island's most successful businesspeople and well-respected by both its bohemian residents and city fathers.

Joe returned and took our orders, and Bernard leaned across the table and asked Joy how she enjoyed the service. I thought it was an awkward question with the preacher in hearing range.

"Bernard," Joy said, "I thought it was inspiring."

Dude leaned toward Joy. "Be good as other preachin' you been to?"

I realized that Dude didn't know anything about Joy and the reason she was staying at Hope House. I wanted to tell him what'd happened but didn't want her story and where-abouts known outside a limited group of people.

Charles decided that Dude was someone we could trust, and said, "Dude, Joy has amnesia and can't remember much about her past."

Dude tapped Joy on the arm and said, "Cool. You be lucky, bad history gone."

Joy's eyes darted around the table, most likely, hoping someone would comment. No one did, and she said, "Thanks, Dude. I think. I wish it was a cool thing. All it makes me think is that I'm an outcast here."

"Cool," Dude said, repeating one of his favorite words.

I was pleased when Joy said, "Why?"

He pointed to each person at the table. "We all outcasts. You be in good company. Cool."

I wouldn't have put it like that, but the truth was that each of us were either outsiders to Folly, or in the cases of Charles and Dude who'd been here many years, were considered left of quirky, even by Folly standards.

Our comments appeared to put Joy at ease and she asked Lottie what'd brought her to Folly. Lottie hesitated before sharing her story, a story involving physical and emotional abuse, and homelessness. Bernard jumped in the conversation and talked about his experiences in Afghanistan, and how he'd been homeless.

Dude had never been homeless or abused, yet felt he needed to add something and said, "Me have Pluto."

As farfetched as it may seem, Joy didn't understand what he was talking about, and said, "You have a planet?"

Dude shook his head and pointed to the ceiling. "Pluto up there be dwarf planet, not planet."

"Oh," Joy said in response to Dude, as many others had said before her.

He pointed to his chest. "Australian Terrier be my Pluto."

Joy grinned. "Oh, they're so cute."

I wondered how she knew that. Clearly, there was much I could learn about amnesia.

Food arrived, and Burl asked for a moment of silence

while he offered a prayer. The noise was getting louder in the crowded restaurant and our table was the only island of silence. The comforting aroma of lunch permeated the area. Burl finished the prayer, and Joy looked at her plate and slowly turned back to Dude, and said, "Dude, what if I have a dog? If I do, who's taking care of it?"

Dude swallowed his first bite of food, and said, "Me be flummoxed."

Charles said, "I'm sure that if you have a dog, it's being taken care of."

I wondered why he was sure.

The conversation turned to what everyone was doing between now and Christmas and Burl shared stories about his younger days growing up on a cattle ranch in southern Illinois. Joy appeared to drift in and out of the conversation and I wondered how difficult it must be for her listening to stories about past Christmases.

Most of us were laughing at something Bernard had said when I noticed Joy staring at the bar along the side of the restaurant. I said, "Joy, what are you thinking?"

She shook her head like she was trying to move back to the present and nodded toward the bar. "Chris, that looks so familiar."

"Like you've been in here before?"

She closed her eyes and said, "Maybe."

Chapter 10

It turned out to be a pleasant Sunday afternoon. Puffy white clouds dotted the blue sky, and the temperature hovered in the low-fifties. Instead of heading home, I turned on Center Street and started toward Barb's Books, when I noticed Joy hurrying to catch up with me. I made a benign comment about how nice the weather was. She asked where I was going, and I told her the bookstore.

"Would you mind if I tag along? I haven't seen Barb since, umm, you know."

"Sure," I said, not waiting for her to relive the traumatic event in the surf.

"Everyone at the house is so nice. Preacher Burl and Adrienne found me some clothes, and, well, they're kind." We walked a few more steps, and she added, "You know what they can't do?"

"What?"

"Give me my memories. I need to get out and get some fresh air to clear my head, at least the little that's in it."

Two men wearing shorts were leaving the bookstore as we approached. They turned in our direction, pivoted, and walked the other way.

Joy shivered and said, "Aren't those guys freezing?"

"I'd be if I had on shorts," I said, and held the door open for Joy.

Barb saw us and smiled. "Hey, Joyce, it's great to see you. Who's that old geezer with you?"

Joy laughed, louder than I thought necessary, and said, "Picked him up on the street. You know him?"

Barb said, "Seen him around. He's not important, how are you?"

"Physically, I'm okay except for a couple of bruises. Can't say the same about my memory."

Barb nodded. "Nothing coming back?"

Joy shook her head.

"Can I offer you something to drink? Coffee, soft drink, water?"

"Coffee would be nice. I'm not as warm blooded as those guys in shorts."

Barb led us to the tiny office behind the showroom. "Oh, did you meet Troy and Nate?"

"No," I said. "They went in the other direction."

Barb said, "They're from Canada, Ottawa, I believe. They think it's hot here."

The names sounded familiar. "Are they your next-door renters?"

"Good memory, Chris." Barb turned to Joy. "Joyce, they're staying next to me in my condo building. They're here for a month."

Joy returned the smile and said, "Preacher Burl started calling me Joy instead of Joyce. I sort of like it."

"Then Joy it is."

Joy's smile faded. "Those guys are here for a month. I wonder how long I'll be here?"

Barb inserted a K-cup pod in her Keurig coffeemaker and turned to Joy. "It'll work out."

Joy turned from looking at the coffeemaker to staring at Barb. "What makes you so certain?"

"From what I've heard, you're surrounded by good people at Hope House, and this is a loving community. It may not be quick, but your memory will start returning and everyone will help you with whatever is needed."

"I hope so."

I told Barb who we had lunch with.

She turned to Joy and said Dude was her half-brother.

Joy stared at her and said, "You're kidding."

Barb laughed and gave Joy an abridged version of their relationship.

All Joy said was, "Hmm, half-brother. Guess that's why he only got half of your vocabulary."

Barb laughed again and said, "Joy, Chris may not have told you, I practiced law for many years before opening the bookstore. I even had a client with the same kind of amnesia you have. I've avoided doing legal work since opening the store, but I'll be glad to help you in any legal entanglements you may encounter."

Barb handed Joy a mug of coffee and inserted another pod in the Keurig.

Joy took a sip, and said, "Barb, I don't have any money. I can't—"

"Joy, we'll deal with that when the time comes. Heck, you may be a billionaire and will want to pay me more than I'm worth."

"Or, I could be broke."

Barb smiled. "Then we'll deal with it later."

My phone rang, I answered and instead of Charles saying anything normal like *hi* or *hello*, he screamed, "Where are you?"

I told him.

"We've gotta go. I'll be out front in five minutes."

"Where?"

The word was wasted. He'd hung up.

I returned the phone to my pocket and Barb said, "What?"

"It was Charles."

"I know that. I heard him yelling."

"He wants me to meet him out front."

Barb shook her head. "Then go?"

"Joy, Charles wants me to go somewhere with him."

Barb answered for her. "Go. Joy and I have some catching up to do. I want to tell her more about Dude and the geezer she came in with. We'll be fine."

I opened the door and Charles's Toyota Venza was already in front of the store and blocking the driving lane. Two cars behind him were patiently waiting for him to move. A third vehicle wasn't as patient and tapped the horn twice. I slid in the passenger seat before road rage commenced, and Charles turned right at the next inter-section.

"Would it be too much to ask where we're going and why the hurry?"

"Nope," he said and kept his eye on the narrow road.

Two blocks later, my question about our destination was answered. Charles pulled in Dude's front yard and parked beside his rusting, green Chevrolet El Camino. The front of the pre-Hugo, elevated, wood-frame house had old-fashioned, multi-colored Christmas lights strung around the front door, up the corners of the house and across the roofline. Straggly shrubs on each side of the steps were covered with more of the near-antique lights.

Before getting out, Charles smacked the steering wheel and said, "Pluto's vamoosed."

Dude must've seen us arrive. He scampered out the front door, down the steps, and was standing at the driver's window motioning for Charles to get out.

"He be gone!" Dude shouted as we exited the car.

Charles put his arm around the distressed, aging hippie. "Let's go in and you can tell us about it."

"What's to tell. He be gone!"

Charles nudged Dude up the steps, and I followed.

This was the second time I'd been in Dude's abode, so I'd gotten over the surprise of seeing wall-to-wall, bright-green shag carpet and the three colorful beanbag chairs arranged in a triangle. Charles helped lower Dude into the green one. Dude slumped down and stared at a lower half of what appeared to be a rubber Santa Claus the size of a large dog bone on the floor beside the red chair.

"Dude, I know Pluto's gone," I said. "What happened."

Dude turned to the back door and said, "Me be at Logger's. Church lunch."

Charles said, "We were with you, remember?"

I wanted to say, "Charles, shut up, and let him finish." Instead, I said. "Let Dude tell us what happened."

"Me skip home from Logger's. See back door cracked open. Pluto gone ... gone."

Charles said, "Do you think someone broke in and took him?"

"You be detective. That's why I call you."

With an effort I wouldn't have needed twenty years ago, I pushed out of the beanbag chair, and walked to the back door. The lock didn't appear tampered with and there was no evidence of a break in. I looked at Charles and shook my head.

He nodded, and said, "Dude, did you go out the back door when you left for church?"

"Exit front. Ride be parked in front." He rubbed his unshaven face. "Woe, today backwards. Took trash out back, then boogied to church."

"Is it possible that the door didn't close all the way when you left?"

He again rubbed his face. "Possible, affirmative. Likely, not." He shrugged.

"Has Pluto gotten out before?"

Dude stood and started pacing the living room floor. "Never."

I said, "Don't you think he'll come home when he gets hungry?"

"What me think, don't mean what he do. Australian Terriers be bred to boogie after rodents and snakes. Me never be lettin' him out without leash. Never," Dude said and went through the kitchen, grabbed his jacket off a chair, and exited to the large patio.

Charles and I followed and watched Dude as he stared at the back yard. He turned to Charles and said, "Woe, plum forgot. You be detective. Here be clue." He picked up a red rhinestone-studded collar that usually adorned Pluto's neck and handed it to Charles. "Stuck to branch behind *hacienda*."

The collar was fastened. I said, "Dude, was it loose on his neck?"

"Loose enough that he could have snagged it on a branch and pulled it off?" Charles added.

"Could be. Me no want to hurt cute little neck. Kept it loose."

Charles ran his hands around the collar, and said, "So, Pluto could have escaped if the door wasn't closed tight enough, got his collar caught on the branch, and ran away."

Dude stared at Charles. "You be detective. You tell me."

Dude then said he was going to drive around and look for the missing member of his family. Charles and I said we'd do the same. I wasn't nearly as worried about Pluto. I figured when he got hungry, he'd find his way back.

An hour later, we'd driven every road on Folly, had seen several dogs walked by their masters, and stopped to ask each person if he or she had seen Pluto. All, to no avail. My optimism faded.

Charles dropped me at the house and said he was going to ride around longer. I didn't think his luck would change. I called Barb to see how her time with Joy went. She had three customers and said she'd call later. I settled in the recliner in my living room and alternated between rehashing the busy day and snoozing. Snoozing ruled.

Chapter 11

It wasn't yet six-thirty and the sun had faded behind the marsh. Early sunsets were my least-favorite features of December. I sighed as it departed and realized that I hadn't had anything to eat since lunch at Loggerhead's. I also realized that my cupboard was bare, its normal condition, and I didn't want to eat another meal today at a restaurant. I walked next door to Bert's Market, Folly's iconic, eclectic grocery that prides itself on never closing and was the island's go-to place for everything from beer to Band-Aids. Included in that mix was a deli where I ordered a five-cheese panini and was killing time waiting for the sandwich when Chief Cindy LaMond moved behind me and said, "You're not ordering something healthy, are you?"

I smiled and said, "I plead the fifth."

"That answers my question," she said, and looked around to see if anyone was close enough to hear us. No one was, and she continued, "I'm glad I ran into you. I was going to call after I got home, and despite being pooped from an exhausting day at work, I'm going to fix a fine five-course gourmet meal for hubby."

"Picking up a pizza from Woody's?" I said.

Woody's pizza was an institution on Folly and had been feeding visitors and locals for years.

Cindy smiled.

"You were going to call me?" I said to move her past the dinner menu.

"Two reasons. Our search for anything, I mean anything, about Joyce Doe, or Jane Joyce, has come up with a big, fat zero. If I hadn't seen her in person, I'd swear she doesn't exist. Her prints aren't on file anywhere. Unless she lost 127 pounds in the last week and changed her skin color, she's not the 215-pound mother of three who's been reported missing in Moncks Corner. The TV stations ran her photo and we've received zero calls from anyone who has an inkling of who she is."

"Cindy, a few of us had lunch at Loggerhead's after church this morning. Joy came with Burl."

"Good," Cindy interrupted. "Burl will be a good influence. Better than some people I know."

I let her comment go. "While we were there, she stopped paying attention to what was being said and looked at the bar. I asked her what was on her mind and she said that it looked familiar."

"Familiar like she'd been there?"

"That's what I asked. She said maybe."

"Or it could be that any bar may look familiar, and it had nothing to do with Loggerhead's."

"Yes," I said.

BILL NOEL

"So, it doesn't tell us more than she's seen a bar."

"I agree. From what you said about not finding anything about a missing person fitting her description, or anyone calling about her photo on television, do you think she's from outside the area?"

Cindy shook her head. "Either that or she's from another planet. And, speaking of being from another planet, that leads me to the second thing I wanted to talk to you about, your buddy Dude."

The deli clerk handed me my panini, I paid, and followed Cindy outside to her city-owned truck. Charles had often joked that Dude emigrated to earth from another planet, a planet where complete sentences were frowned upon and had a different meaning than they do on earth. This was one of the few times Cindy agreed with Charles.

"What about him?"

"He began calling and pestering me this afternoon about the shorter, more articulate version of him that's missing."

"Dude called you about Pluto?"

"Eventually. Dude first called Mayor Newman, Councilmember Salmon, the preacher at the Baptist Church, Preacher Burl, and then me about his missing canine. Mayor Newman called me and rearranged the priorities of my department from catching bad guys, stopping speeders, and ticketing those law-breaking vacationers who have the audacity to park with a tire or two touching the pavement on our streets. My priority now is finding one lost Australian Terrier. To paraphrase the words of our fine citizen, *Dude be full o clout.*"

I smiled and asked if she's had any luck.

"As much as we've had at learning Joy's identity. Dude

told me that you and Charles were the first on the scene of the canine escape. I was going to call to ask if Dude said anything that made you think that Pluto's disappearance was anything other than the critter wanting to get away from Dude to maintain his sanity. Believe it or not, there are times that I don't fully understand what Dude's talking about. You spend more time with him and other oddball characters than I do, so I figured you might understand him better."

I understood Dude better than I understood thermodynamics although not much better.

"Cindy, Dude's upset."

"Duh."

"Pluto means everything to him. Dude doesn't have many close friends and Pluto is probably his best. He was clueless about how Pluto escaped. I didn't see anything that made me think it was anything other than the dog scampering out the back door that was left ajar. Dude had taken the trash out that way before going to church. Most of the time he leaves by the front door since his car's parked in the front yard. He was carrying trash, so it would've been easy for him to not shut the door all the way."

"That's what I thought but wanted your take. When I was there, the poor boy was near tears. My experience with dogs, and with Larry, is that once hunger sets in, they find their way home. Worry not, all my patrol vehicles are out scouring the island for one missing Australian Terrier. If they happen to stumble across a murder in progress, they may stop, unless they're chasing Pluto. And speaking of dogs, Larry, and hunger, I'd better get home with a pizza before he calls the mayor on me."

I wished her luck, headed home, used my one culinary

skill, and microwaved the panini that'd turned cold while I was talking to Cindy. I also poured a glass of Cabernet, and wondered who Joy was, and to a lesser extent, where Pluto was.

Chapter 12

Christmas was less than a week away although you could hardly tell it from looking at my house, inside or out. I had hooked a ten-year-old, dusty artificial wreath I bought at a yard sale for seventy-five cents on the front door and inside, my decorating was a ceramic Dickens Village Victoria Station setting on a table in the living room. Other than the wreath, the Station was the only item I brought from Kentucky that I associated with Christmas. I'd thought of adding more but rationalized that there was no need since I seldom had anyone to the house and considered the party at Cal's Country Bar and Burgers my prime event on Christmas Day. Looking at the Victoria Station reminded me that it'd been a couple of weeks since I'd talked to Cal, besides a burger sounded good. During the off-season, there was less than a fifty-fifty chance that Cal's would be open for lunch or early beer drinking. I had nothing better to do, so I took a chance and drove the short distance since the outside temperature was near freezing.

The front door was locked. If I wanted food my gamble hadn't paid off, but there was still a chance Cal was inside. I went to the side door and had better luck. The jukebox was playing a Hank Williams Sr. classic, and Cal, who could double as an older, much older, version of Hank, was singing along and sliding a table to the center of the room. My friend was seventy-three-years-old, six-foot-three, razor thin with a spine that curved forward from leaning down to a microphone and living for decades out of the back seat of his car. His long, gray hair inched out from around a Stetson that had travelled with him for forty plus years. I smiled when I saw a strand of battery-operated LED lights strung around the crown, his seasonal addition to the hat. Cal wore a black T-shirt instead of his rhinestone covered white coat he wore when performing. *Ho, Ho, Ho!* was in glittery, silver paint on the front of the T-shirt. His holiday-inspired attire also included bright-red slacks and red tennis shoes. The bar, like Cal, was in a marginal state of repair, yet with its beat-up tables and chairs, indoor/outdoor carpet covered floor, and antique Wurlitzer jukebox, the owner swore it was "the perfect country music bar." Cal would know since he travelled the South for more than four decades singing at any venue that would have him.

Cal saw me in the doorway. He tipped his Stetson in my direction, and said, "Halleluiah! My Christmas wish is answered. An elf has come to help this old codger."

And, all I wanted was a hamburger.

"Help with what?"

He waved his hand around the room. "I'm running late finishing party decorations. It's getting harder and harder each year for me to get everything done. My energy level ain't what it used to be."

I followed his gaze and saw three—yes, three—seven-foot-tall artificial Christmas trees in the room. Their multiple strands of colorful lights matched the strands Cal had attached to each non-moving vertical surface, and more were hanging from the ceiling. Unless Santa was shoveling snow in front of the room while Mrs. Claus was feeding the reindeer, I couldn't imagine how much more could be done to make the bar Christmas-party ready.

"What can I do?"

He pointed to the corner near the front door. "Look over there. There's a wide-open space begging for a Christmas tree."

The corner's apparent cry for help was lost on the man who had a grand total of zero Christmas trees in his house. What wasn't lost on me was Cal's childlike enthusiasm for the holiday and his desire to make his bar reflect his glee.

"Do you have a tree?"

His smile was as wide as his face. "Sure do, and now I have an elf to help put it up."

Not only did he have a tree, he had a six-foot ladder, and enough strands of lights to humiliate the tree in Times Square. As if on cue, Gene Autry's version of "Frosty the Snowman" began on the jukebox. "Frosty" was one of many Christmas songs Cal added each December.

During the lull between Gene Autry's singing and Burl Ives, the singer, not the preacher, telling us about "Rudolph the Red-Nosed Reindeer," Cal said, "Have you and Charles found Pluto?"

"How do you know about Pluto?"

He handed me the strand of lights to hang around the back of the tree. "Let's see. It could've been when Officer Spencer came in last night and said he'd driven around the island 739 times looking for the dog or could've been when Councilmember Salmon stopped by for a brew and said that his wife made him ride around looking. No, I got it, it was when the Dudester charged in the door whistling and yelling, 'Yo, Pluto, you be here?'"

I laughed, and said, "The word's out."

"A woeful understatement, my friend," Cal said, and pulled a chair to the front of the tree and lowered his body in it.

"What makes you think Charles or I may've found Pluto?"

He pointed to a nearby chair. "Take a load off."

We weren't finished with the tree, but Cal was breathing heavily and needed to rest. I pulled the chair close to his and sat.

"Dude said the police would do their best to find the missing family member, but he had more confidence that you and especially Charles would find him since your buddy was a professional detective."

"He said all that?"

"Not those words, but that's my interpretation of what he was trying to say."

"To my knowledge, neither Charles nor anyone else has found Pluto. I haven't talked to Dude today, so the pup might be safe and cuddled up to his master."

Cal removed his Stetson and set it on the floor beside the chair. "Then let me ask you this," he said. "Figured out who that Joy gal is that you and Miss Barb found surfin' at the County Park?"

"How do you know about Joy?"

"I hope you don't want me to name everyone who told

me about her? There've been a dozen or so guys and gals in here talking about it."

"What've you heard?"

"About you finding her? About where she's staying? Or, about what happened to her memory?"

"All of them."

He told me what he knew about Barb and me finding her, and where she was staying. He was one-hundred percent accurate. When it came to what happened to her memory, the percent dropped drastically. The consensus was that she'd been clobbered with a steel pipe and left on the beach. Theories about who clobbered her included her husband, someone robbing her, the jealous wife of someone who was cheating with Joy, and an alien who'd parked his/her/it's spaceship in the County Park because of its wide-open space. Cal said he didn't put much faith in the alien option. Unfortunately, the accuracy of where she was staying was dead on. That shoots the idea that if someone is after her, the fewer people who knew where she was the better.

He exhausted everything he knew about Joy and was rejuvenated and anxious to finish decorating the tree. Frank Sinatra was singing "Jingle Bells," as Cal pushed himself out of the chair and pointed for me to get back on the ladder so he could give me the final strand of lights.

"Chris," he said as I wrapped the lights around the top of the tree, "remember when I told you why my Christmas party was so important?"

"Wasn't it three years ago when you had the first one?"

"Four."

"Time flies. You said it was because you'd spent many

Christmases on the road and most of those years you didn't have anywhere to go to celebrate the holiday. You'd met others in the same boat."

"Yeah, I told myself that if I ever had a place where I could throw a party for everyone who wanted to come, regardless if they had a family, were homeless, had any money, whatever, that I'd do it." He smiled and pointed to each tree. "Being able to do this makes me happier than anything I do all year. People are saying this'll be the biggest."

I'd been to most of his Christmas parties and the number attending had increased dramatically.

The sound of Bing Crosby singing "White Christmas" filled the room.

Cal hooked a large ornament on the tree and pointed to the jukebox. "My favorite Christmas song."

He'd told me that last year. I was thinking how strange it was that I'd remembered that bit of trivia when I couldn't remember what I had for lunch two days ago.

He interrupted my thought when he said, "I have three versions on the jukebox: Bing, Eddy Arnold, and Loretta Lynn." He hesitated, glanced at the new tree, and then at the jukebox, and joined Bing singing, "I'm dreaming of a white Christmas, just like the ones I used to know." He turned to me. "Chris, think about how bad it'll be for poor Joy on Sunday. She won't be able to remember anything about the ones she used to know. Christmases with friends, with families, maybe with children. How lonely and sad must that be?"

I'd thought about her lack of memory about family and friends but hadn't thought of it in relation to Christmas. "You're right."

"Chris, ain't nothing I can do about her past and those memories. If you can get her to the party, we'll give her a Christmas she'll remember for a long time."

"I'll see what I can do."

Chapter 13

I left my car at Cal's and walked two blocks to the surf shop to see if Dude's wayward child had returned. The surf shop, with its name in all lower case for reasons known only to Dude, was a gold mine during vacation season. In the winter, its owner spent days in the Lost Dog Cafe drinking tea and bemoaning how bad business was. He seldom got sympathy from the less-successful business owners.

To my chagrin, I was met by Stephon instead of Dude. Stephon was rude and snarky. I'd learned to tolerate his condescending attitude, and he tolerated me to the point that he didn't become hostile when he saw me. Dude kept him on the payroll because he was a surfer and magically meshed with the store's more offbeat customers.

"Good afternoon, Stephon," I said in the most civil tone I could muster. "Is Dude around?"

The clerk was rearranging a rack of wetsuits and wasn't going to let my arrival distract him. "No."

"Is he at the Lost Dog Cafe?"

"No."

"Do you know where he is?"

"No."

This was one of my more civil conversations with Stephon, so I decided to quit while I was ahead.

"Thanks."

I turned to leave, and was surprised to hear, "He's looking for Pluto."

I stopped and looked at the employee who'd turned from the wetsuits and was staring at me. I motioned for him to continue.

"I've never seen boss man so upset. I don't know why, but he likes you. Maybe you can try to find him and help him search. Don't tell him I said this." He looked around and lowered his voice like he was about to tell me the combination to Dude's safe. "You could put your arm around the boss man and say it'll be okay. I would, except you may not know this, but I'm not much at warm and fuzzy. When you asked if I knew where he was, I said no because I don't. Oh yeah, one more thing, when you find him, don't say anything about the Lost Dog Cafe. He might start whimpering if he hears the words lost dog. He's walking the streets. Please help him."

Where was my recorder when I needed it? I said I would and heard two words I didn't know were in Stephon's vocabulary. "Thank you."

The odds on me finding Dude if I walked would be near zero and the temperature felt nearly that cold, so I returned to Cal's and got the car and started my canvas of the island. I was surprised that Pluto hadn't ventured home on his own. I started on Dude's street and drove a grid for fifteen minutes. I saw two couples walking dogs and stopped to ask if they'd seen Dude or a lost Australian Terrier. Each said they hadn't seen Pluto but had talked with Dude who stopped them and asked if they'd seen his missing buddy.

I was about to give up my search when I spotted the surf shop owner in front of Hope House talking with Preacher Burl. I stopped and joined them. Dude wore a stoplight-red unzipped parka revealing his tie-dyed T-shirt with a peace symbol on the front, jeans with a rip in each knee, red driving gloves, and hiking boots. He held the leash with the rhinestone-studded collar dangling Pluto-less. He looked more like he was hiking the Appalachian Trail than looking for his pet. He also wore a frown.

"No luck," I said.

Dude shook his head and Burl patted him on the back and said, "We're putting together a search party to help Brother Dude. Brother Bernard and Sister Joy are robing themselves in heavier clothing and Sister Rebekah should arrive any minute. She had to wait for someone to relieve her at Black Magic." Burl held up his phone. "I'm coordinating the search."

"Chrisster, my poor baby could be frozen like a popsicle."

The temperature was well above freezing although it didn't feel it, so I doubted Pluto could have frozen, but it wouldn't do any good to share that observation.

Joy and Bernard joined us, and Burl asked if I was going to help search. Dude looked at me with sad eyes, so I said, "Of course."

Burl said, "Okay, here's the plan. Brother Bernard, you know the island pretty well." Burl pointed east. "Why don't you head off that way? Brother Dude, why don't you go toward town and check behind shops and restaurants? Pluto should be hungry and there are plenty of places where he could root in the trash for food."

Bernard said, "Dude, if you want, I can tell you the best trash cans for food."

Bernard was talking from experience after having been homeless for many months and searching for food and warmth wherever possible.

Dude said, "Okeydokey."

"Sister Joy, you're new here so why don't you go with Brother Chris? That way you'll learn more about the island and will help Chris look while he focuses on driving."

Joy glanced at me, and I said, "Good idea."

"Good," Burl said. "When Sister Rebekah gets here, I'll recommend that she looks west of Center Street."

Joy was quiet the first few minutes of our search. The coat Burl found for her was several sizes too large and she had a challenging time getting comfortable in the seat with the seatbelt and bulky overgarment. She finally took it off and threw it in the backseat. I carried the conversation and tried to point out some sites and homes where I knew the residents.

"Chris," she finally said, "I don't know who my friends were before, well, you know."

"Yes."

She shook her head. "I don't know if I have a family."

"I understand."

"Let me tell you what I do know. Preacher Burl and the others in the house have been fantastic. They're from diverse backgrounds. They've had ups and downs, mostly downs, I'm saddened to learn. Despite that, they've been wonderful. They seem to truly care. I hope that if, no, when,

I regain my memory, my past has that many good people in it."

"I do too."

The heater was pumping out hot air full-blast, but she was shivering. I didn't think it was because she was cold since she'd removed the coat.

I said, "Want some coffee?"

She smiled. "That sounds good."

I pulled in a parallel parking space at the side of Bert's Market and asked if she wanted to go in with me. She said sure, grabbed the coat from the back seat, and followed me to the coffee urn. Two men were putting sugar in cups. I didn't recognize them at first, and then it hit me. They were Barb's temporary neighbors. One of them noticed me standing behind them and said, "Oh, sorry. Let us get out of your way."

He stepped aside and pulled the other man with him.

"Hi," I said, "I'm Chris, and this is my friend, Joy. Aren't you Barb Deanelli's new neighbors?"

"Yes," the taller of the two said. "How'd you know?"

I explained that I'd seen them coming out of Barb's Books and she told me who they were.

"Oh. I'm Troy and this is Nate."

Troy shook my hand and nodded to Joy. Nate stood back and didn't seem interested in talking to us.

"You're from Canada," I said, to end the awkward silence.

"Yes," Troy said.

"Troy, we'd better get going," Nate said and took a step toward the door.

Troy shook his head. "Nate's always in a hurry. Nice meeting you Chris. You too, Joy. Pretty name."

She mumbled, "Thank you."

Barb's neighbors were gone, we got our coffee, and I asked Joy if she wanted anything to eat. She said no, and we continued our search. Over the next hour we saw dogs of assorted sizes, breeds, and colors. Not one was named Pluto.

"Joy, Sunday when we were eating at Loggerhead's, you said the bar looked familiar. Did anything else about it come back to you?"

"I thought about it all night. Nothing. You asked if I'd been there before. I still don't know. Sorry."

"That's okay."

I drove out East Ashley Avenue to Thirteenth Street. I didn't think Pluto would have wandered that far but had an idea. I turned on Tabby Drive and past the house with *Caulder* painted in script on a piece of driftwood on the wall beside the front door. The driveway was empty, so I figured no one was home. I asked Joy to follow me to the back yard. She gave me a strange look but followed me to the walking pier that led to the eighteen-foot-long runabout that had been returned to its owners.

"Chris, did you see Pluto?"

I walked to the end of the pier and put my hand on the Tahoe's stern. "No. I was wondering if this boat means anything to you?"

She looked at it and at me. "No, why should ... oh, is this the one that was stolen, the one you think I was on?"

I nodded.

She pulled her coat tighter and returned her gaze to the watercraft. She leaned over and looked in the boat and stepped back and looked at its side.

"I know it would be good if I recognized it, but I don't."

It was worth a try. "Ready to get back on Pluto patrol?"

She nodded, and we headed to the car. Before she stepped off the pier, she looked back at the boat, stopped, slowly shook her head, and whispered, "Sorry."

Forty-five minutes later, we'd covered most every street on the island, some more than once, and decided that if Pluto was wandering around, one of the many searchers would have found him. I was beginning to think that the poor dog had suffered a fate that none of us had imagined, a fate that would devastate Dude. I didn't share that thought with Joy or Burl who was waiting for us. Bernard had already returned and was in the living room sipping on a mug of coffee. Burl offered cups to Joy and me which we quickly accepted. He said that Rebekah was in her room resting after working all morning at Black Magic and traipsing around looking for Pluto. Dude had phoned Burl and said he wasn't stopping until sunset and thanked us for our efforts. Burl went to the kitchen to get more coffee.

"Chris," Joy said during a break in the conversation about Pluto, "who again were those men you talked to in Bart's?"

"Bert's," I corrected, sounding like Charles. "They're Barb's neighbors. She told us about them when we were in the bookstore the other day?"

"I remember. It's just, I wondered if you knew anything else about them."

"No, why?"

"Nothing specific. It's like how the bar in Loggerhead's looked familiar. They're vaguely familiar. I've probably seen them around town, that's all."

Burl returned to the living room and said, "Chris, will you be joining us for our Christmas Eve service?"

"I plan to, why?"

"Curious. What about Christmas Day?"

"Of course."

"Good."

Then I remembered what Cal had said about Joy coming to his party. "Preacher, will you be at Cal's Christmas party? I remember you had an enjoyable time there last year."

Burl smiled, "Brother Chris, I had a wonderful time until Brother Cal dragged me on stage and made me sing a duet with him. I could've crawled under a table."

"Preacher, you were good. Joy, our friend Cal has a big party each Christmas. I know he'd love for you to come."

"I don't know. Everyone will be a stranger, and—"

Bernard interrupted, "Bologna, Joy. You'll be among friends, lots of them. You'll see. Last year was the first time I went. That's when I talked to Preacher Burl and he helped me, helped me a bunch."

She smiled. "Maybe I'll give it a try."

That would do for now.

Chapter 14

The weather gurus predicted Tuesday would be the best day of the week, so I took advantage of the warm, dry morning and walked two blocks to Rita's Seaside Grille at the corner of Center Street and East Arctic Avenue. The restaurant was on its third name since I'd moved to Folly and was conveniently located across the street from the Folly Pier, catty-corner from the nine-story, oceanfront Tides Hotel, and across Center Street from the iconic Sand Dollar Social Club. The lunch-hour was a few minutes away, and I had the choice of a table or a booth. My preference would have been a table on the patio, but even though today was to be the pick of the week, it was too cool to sit outside. I chose a booth along the sidewalk side of the colorful restaurant and quickly drew the attention of Samantha, a server who'd waited on me several times over the years. She asked if I wanted a menu and I told her I knew what I wanted.

She grinned and said, "Cheeseburger, medium rare?"

I smiled and nodded.

"One of these days you're going to order something different and I'll have to call the *Folly Current*, so they can do a story on the alien who invaded Chris Landrum's body." She turned and headed toward the kitchen.

While I waited for my predictable cheeseburger to arrive, I wondered if Dude had found Pluto. I started to dial his number when Charles bounded through the entry and headed my way.

"Thought that was your bald head shining in the window." He slid into the seat opposite me. "You already ordered your cheeseburger?"

"Good morning, Charles."

"There you go. Trying to introduce civility. When are you going to give up and start talking like your friends?"

I was beginning to wonder that myself when Samantha reappeared with my lunch and asked Charles if he wanted anything.

"Sam, I'm glad you asked. All morning I've had a hankering for world peace, a cure for the common cold, and a grouper sandwich."

"We can't fry up the first two, Charles, but the grouper sandwich is a no-brainer for the chef."

"I'll settle for that."

"So," Charles said as Samantha went in search of a grouper sandwich, "what's the latest on Pluto?"

"I was going to call Dude when you invited yourself to lunch."

Charles nodded toward my phone on the corner of the table. "What's stopping you?"

You, I wanted to say. Instead, I tapped the speaker icon,

so Charles could listen, and then tapped on Dude's number and waited through six rings before his voicemail message said, "Be lookin' for pup Pluto. Unless you know where he be, don't waste time leavin' words."

I didn't know where Pluto was, so I didn't leave a message.

Charles stared at the phone. "Dude says more words on his voicemail message than he uses in person."

I shared how I, and several others, had spent hours yesterday looking for the lost canine. Charles said he knew because he ran into Dude snooping around Charles's apartment building looking for you know what. Charles then spent an hour walking the streets in his part of the island, to no avail.

Samantha told Charles his food would be out shortly, before she leaned over the table and said, "Any word on Dude's dog?"

"No," Charles said. "How did you hear about Pluto?"

She shook her head. "Do I look deaf and blind?"

"No," Charles said, in an astute observation.

"Everybody knows about Pluto. Dude was in here twice last night asking if anyone had seen an Australian Terrier hanging around. Those weren't his exact words. A couple from New Jersey looked at him funny, but most of us knew what he was talking about and said we hadn't seen the poor creature." She then said she'd better get Charles's lunch and headed to the kitchen.

Charles shared a couple of stories he'd heard about a restaurant closing on Folly Road and about a book he'd been reading about Herbert Hoover. I covered my mouth, so he wouldn't see my yawn of boredom. I said, "Interesting."

He detected my level of disinterest in his choice of books, and said, "Chris, I'm beginning to think something bad happened to Pluto. If he'd hopped, skipped, and jumped away on his own, don't you think he would've found his way home or some of us would have seen him?"

I nodded, and Samantha set Charles's lunch in front of him and moved to the next booth to see if a father and his two young kids were ready to order.

Charles took a bite and mumbled, "Think he's dead?"

"I'm not ready to go there. Someone could've taken him in and planned to keep him. He's cute and friendly."

"Yes, but he's Dude's."

"We know that. He didn't have a collar, so he could've been mistaken for a stray."

Charles took another bite, nodded left and then right, and said, "Think we should start knocking on doors and asking if anyone has a new pet?"

"I don't know."

"We need to do something, if we—"

I interrupted Charles and stood to greet Joy who was headed our way.

"I thought it was you, Chris," she said and smiled.

"You saw his bald head in the window, didn't you?" Charles said and scooted over and offered her a seat.

"No, I recognized him." She looked at the spot Charles had vacated for her, hesitated, and said, "Do you mind if I join you?"

I was pleased that she asked even after Charles moved over. I said, "We'd be honored."

Samantha returned and asked the newcomer if she wanted something to eat or drink.

Joy looked at Charles's plate, then at mine, and said, "I don't have any... I don't think—"

Charles interrupted and said, "Go ahead and get something. It's on Chris."

Thanks, Charles.

She looked at me and I smiled. "Maybe I'll have what Chris has."

Samantha said it was an excellent choice and once again headed to the kitchen.

Charles said, "Out for a walk?"

"Sort of. Still looking for Pluto. Dude came by early this morning and asked if we could help him look. The poor man was near tears. That dog means a lot to him."

"It's his family," Charles said.

I chose not to mention that Pluto wasn't Dude's entire family since Barb was his half-sister.

Joy looked out the window and at the bartender pulling a beer out of the cooler behind the bar along the other side of the room. "Wonder if I have pets."

I said, "Do pets sound familiar? Is anything coming back?"

She continued to look at the bar and instead of answering my question, said, "Pets, no." She rubbed her eyes and continued to look at the bar. "Chris, why does that look familiar?"

I looked at the bar. "The bar, the bartender, or what?"

"The bar."

This was the second bar that she'd said looked familiar. "Does it look more familiar than the one in Loggerhead's?"

"I don't know." She shook her head. "There's something about it." She exhaled and said. "Don't you think I want to know what it is?"

Charles patted her arm. "It's okay, Joy. We'll figure it out. Won't we, Chris?"

Thanks again, Charles. "We'll do what we can."

She attempted a smile and failed.

Samantha returned with a real smile and Joy's cheeseburger. She asked if we needed anything else. I was tempted to say a memory for Joy. I resisted and thanked her.

Joy took a large bite, and I wondered if it was the first thing she'd had to eat today. Charles asked how she liked staying at Hope House.

"It's okay. Everyone is nice."

"How's your room?" Charles asked, mainly to get her mind off worrying about the past.

"Great. Preacher Burl says I have the best room in the house."

"That's great," Charles said. "The preacher is a great person."

Joy started to put a fry in her mouth, hesitated, and returned it to the plate. "Chris, I don't have a right to, but could I ask a big favor?"

"Sure."

"Would you to take me back to that boat you said I was on?"

"Of course, we will," Charles answered for me.

We, I thought. "Joy, do you remember something about the boat?"

"I might. I woke up in the middle of the night thinking about it. I was half dreaming, half awake, so I'm not sure what was what. If I see it when I'm awake, something might click."

"If you want, we can go after we finish here."

"Good idea," Charles said, answering for Joy.

It could have been my imagination, but Joy finished lunch quicker than she'd started. Charles was waving for Samantha to bring me the check before any of us had finished our sandwiches.

Chapter 15

We walked to my house with Charles stopping every few steps to holler Pluto and look for the elusive canine behind every structure. It took nearly as long to walk the short distance as it did to eat lunch.

"I like where you live," Joy said, as we approached my car in the drive. "It's cute. Lived here long?"

"Almost as long as I've been on Folly."

"Could use more Christmas decorations," Charles said as he pointed to the lonely wreath on the door.

We piled in the car before Charles, the man who had no Christmas decorations on his apartment, could tell me how to exterior decorate my cottage. The two-mile ride out East Ashley Avenue took longer than man's first flight to the moon. Charles had me pull over at each beach access walkway, so he could get out and yell for Pluto. We also had to stop at each house that had more Christmas decorations than my wreath, so Charles could show me how I could decorate my humble abode. I could tell that Joy was getting impatient, but since we were doing her a favor, she held her annoyance. I wasn't as accommodating and ignored Charles' last five requests to stop. Our next stop was in front of the Caulder residence.

Fortunately, the house didn't have as much Christmas decorations as did mine, nor were there any vehicles in the drive. Charles was quick to exit and was nearly to the boat before Joy and I got out. The only witnesses to our trespassing were a dozen pelicans perched on a pier two houses away. Joy was staring at the boat through the window and didn't appear like she wanted to get closer.

"Are you okay, Joy?"

She jerked back from the window.

"Sorry to startle you, you okay?"

She whispered, "I don't know."

"Want to go home?"

She said something I couldn't understand. I leaned closer and asked her to repeat it.

"I think so."

"I'll get Charles."

I walked halfway to the pier and called for Charles who was leaning over the boat looking like he was about to climb aboard. I waved for him to return to the car until I noticed Joy opening the door and walking my way.

She was tiptoeing like she was on broken glass, and said, "You brought me out here and I need to look in the boat. Honest, I do."

Charles shrugged, pointed to the boat, and then at the car.

I put my arm around Joy and led her toward Charles.

The temperature was mild, the sun was out in all its glory, and she had on her oversized coat, yet was shivering.

Charles moved away from the craft and let Joy look over the gunwale. She continued to shiver, and I kept my arm around her waist. She stared for just shy of an eternity, before saying, "I was back there."

Charles moved up beside us and looked in the back of the boat. "In the back seat?"

Joy nodded.

I tightened my grip on her, and said, "What do you remember?"

She closed her eyes, and said, "The boat moving fast. Bouncing in the waves. I'm on my stomach on that seat. My head hit the seat every wave. It hurt." She opened her eyes and pointed at the white with blue trim, fold-down back seat. She looked at her left wrist and massaged it with her right hand. "Tied with a rope. Got it loose. Untied my feet. He didn't look back." She continued to look at her wrist.

I waited for her to continue. Charles, who hadn't perfected the art of patience, said, "You were tied up and on the back seat. Then what?"

She looked at him like it was the first time she noticed him standing beside us. "Then nothing." She shook her head. "Nothing."

Charles said, "Are you sure that—"

Joy interrupted, "Can we leave?"

I said yes and moved beside her as she walked off the pier. We got in the car and slowly turned around at the end of the dead-end street and headed to town. Joy remained silent until we were in front of Hope House.

"Thank you for taking me. Sorry I couldn't remember more."

"That's okay. It's coming back."

"Joy," Charles said, "when you were talking about being on the boat, you said, 'He didn't look back.' Do you remember anything about him?"

"No."

I said, "Was there only one person?"

"There could've been more. I only remember the one sitting behind the wheel in front of me."

"And you can't remember anything about him?" Charles said. "What he was wearing. If he had a hat on, or if you could you see the color of his hair. Did he say anything?"

"I don't remember."

"You're doing fine, Joy," I said. "Tell you what, if you remember more about being on the boat or the man, or if there was someone with him, would you give me a call? I can let the police know so they can follow up."

"Okay," she said, and thanked us again for lunch and for taking her to see the boat.

I pulled in Charles's gravel parking lot and waited for him to say something about Joy. He'd been unusually silent since we'd left her.

"Chris," he finally spoke, "I don't know what to make of it. I don't understand amnesia. How could she have been in that boat and then get off the boat and float to shore on a surfboard without remembering anything about it?"

I was no expert on retrograde amnesia but knew it was real. Joy had no reason to fake it. Slices of her memory are coming back, and if Barb was correct, most, if not all, will eventually return.

I shared my limited knowledge with Charles, and added, "I'm more worried about her safety. Whether it be one, two, or more people who took her out on the boat, it was against her will and I can only imagine what he, or they, had intended."

Charles added, "Dump her in the ocean, never to be seen again, alive, that is."

I nodded.

"You're afraid whoever it was will try again?"

"Yes. Despite the best efforts to keep her whereabouts secret, too many people know where she's living."

"That's why we have to figure out who and stop them from causing more harm."

I rolled my eyes. "That's why the *police* need to solve it— emphasis on police."

"Whatever. That's why you're going to pick up your phone and call Chief LaMond and tell her what we heard about Joy and the boat."

I thought about waiting until I got in the comfort of my home before calling and being the recipient of her wrath about me nosing in police business. Why not let Charles suffer with me? I called the Chief's cell phone and hit the speaker icon.

Cindy answered with, "Happy almost Christmas, Mr. Landrum."

Her pleasant comment threw me, and Charles stared at the phone like it was a scorpion.

"You're in a good mood," I said.

"Aren't I always?"

"No."

"Well, aren't you a damned Debbie downer? Get in the Christmas spirit. Take me, for example. I'm standing in this hoity-toity jewelry store in downtown Charleston with my lovey-dovey hubby and trying on an antique gold ring with a beryl stone and a cute little diamond on each side of it."

"Beryl?" I said.

"Light-blue gemstone, my jewelry-challenged friend. Enough about the exquisite ring lovey-dovey is getting me for Christmas. Why have you called to ruin my perfectly wonderful, and I might add, historic, day when hubby takes me jewelry shopping?"

"Charles and I were having lunch with Joy and she asked us to take her to the boat on Tabby Drive."

"Why?" she interrupted.

Charles leaned close to the phone and said, "Because we were hungry."

"Why'd she ask you to take her to the boat, Chris, who now sounds a lot like Charles, that moronic friend of yours?"

Enough foolishness, I thought. "She hoped it would bring back memories."

Cindy sighed. "Did it?"

I shared what Joy had remembered. Cindy asked twice if she said anything about the man in the boat other than he was sitting behind the wheel. Twice, I answered she hadn't.

"What am I supposed to do with that modicum of near-worthless information?"

"Modicum?" Charles said.

"Itsy, teeny-weeny bit," she said.

I was ready to hang up on the chief and throw Charles out of the car, when Cindy added, "Thanks, Chris. It's not much but it confirms that Joy was on the boat, and most likely, in the ocean. The who, what, and why are yet to be determined. Any word on Pluto?"

That kind of abrupt transition was a hallmark of Charles, but not foreign to several of my friends.

"Not that I've heard."

"Me either," Charles added to not be left out.

"Larry has another gem for me to try on. Better go. He only gets in this generous mood every... umm, never."

She ended the call after agreeing to let me know if she learned anything or if Pluto was found. And, at her urging, I agreed to let her know before I got killed playing cop.

Chapter 16

I walked to Bert's to get prepackaged doughnuts for breakfast. It was four days until Christmas and Bert's employees' shirts reflected the holiday. Two guys hard at work behind the deli counter wore red T-shirts, one with a picture of Santa on the front and the other with the head of a smiling reindeer. Mary Ewing was stocking a shelf near the back of the store and smiled when she saw me. She had on a red and white Santa's hat and a green sweatshirt with *Merry Christmas* on the front. When I met Mary a year ago, she was anorexic thin with dirty blond hair. Since then, she'd added twenty pounds to her five-foot-five frame and her hair was clean and pulled in a ponytail. She looked fresh and younger than her mid-twenties.

Her smile lit up the room. "Good morning, Mr. Landrum."

"Mary, you know to call me Chris. Ready for the big day?"

She gave me a hug, stepped back, and continued to

smile. "I'd better be. Jewel and Joanie are counting the hours until Santa arrives."

The single mother and high-school dropout was struggling last Christmas to find somewhere warm to spend the nights with her girls. Preacher Burl heard of their situation, found them a place to live, got Mary the job at Bert's, and gave them hope. He also got her enrolled in a GED program where she could work toward her high-school equivalency diploma.

I remembered how excited Joanie and Jewel were last Christmas to get something as simple as new clothes for the holiday. "I bet they're excited."

A customer interrupted our conversation to ask Mary where to find ketchup. Mary smiled and walked the woman to the condiments and returned to where I was looking at the packaged sweets, a.k.a. breakfast.

"They're super excited. This'll be the first Christmas for Jewel in a house where we're actually living."

"That's wonderful."

"I almost forgot," Mary said and tapped the side of her head. "I met someone you know."

"Who?"

"Joy. She said you and your lady friend saved her life."

"Barb and I were in the right place at the right time. Where did you meet her?"

"Yesterday, after work, Joanie, Jewel, and I were walking along the beach. It was windy and cold, but when my gals want to walk on the beach, nothing can stop them. We were bundled up and saw Joy walking toward us. She was wrapped up in a big coat and looking at the pier. You know Joanie's never met a stranger, so she went over to Joy." Mary laughed and shook her head. "Joanie said, 'I'm excited about Christmas. How about you?'"

That sounded like Joanie. I smiled, and said, "What did Joy say?"

"She knelt and smiled at Joanie. I didn't think there was much happiness behind her smile, anyway, she said she was excited and asked Joanie her name. You know, that's all it took. Joanie not only told the stranger her name but pointed to Jewel and me and shared our names, where we lived, and how much we were looking forward to Christmas. She finally got around to asking the lady who she was. She told us she was Joy." Mary chuckled. "Joanie is obsessed with words, something she's getting from school, I suppose. She pointed to her sister, at Joy, and then at herself, and said, 'That's funny. All our names start with *J*.' That got an honest smile from Joy."

"How'd you learn that Joy knew me?"

"My busybody seven-year-old. After she figured out the *J* names, she asked Joy if she lived on Folly. Joy said she guessed she did. That did it. Joanie asked what Joy meant by guessed she lived here. Joanie said something like, 'Don't you know where you live?' Joy told her it was hard to understand, but that you and Barbara found her, and she was now staying at Hope House. Joanie knows about the house and that it was started by that wonderful man, Preacher Burl. I interrupted Joanie's interrogation of the poor lady who'd been minding her business and walking on the beach. I told Joanie we needed to get going and to let the lady continue her walk."

"That was nice of Joanie to talk to Joy."

"Yes. Joy said it was nice meeting us and that she looked

forward to seeing us again. I told her that you and I were friends. I hope that was okay."

I told her it was. Mary said she didn't know anything about Joy but that she was going to stop by to visit her. I said it was a good idea. Another customer asked Mary a question, and I told her that I didn't want to keep her from work.

I grabbed some coffee, paid for breakfast, headed home, and thought how it would be good for both Mary and Joy to get better acquainted, or, knowing as little as I did about Joy, thought it would be good.

I tore open the package of doughnuts and started breakfast when the phone rang.

"I was thinking," Charles said to open the conversation.

"Might I ask what?" I said before stuffing one of the treats in my mouth.

"You might," Charles said, and laughed.

I waited for him to tell me instead of asking again.

"You're no fun. Why don't you come pick me up and I'll not only tell you, I'd do a show-and-tell, and we can see if I'm right."

The logical thing to do would be to ask what he might be right about, or moving past that, suggest that he pick me up. He had a car, and it was his idea. Logical and Charles seldom coexisted. I told him I'd be at his place in fifteen minutes.

"Where are we going?" I asked as he got in the car. I thought it was an appropriate question since all Charles had said was for me to pick him up.

"East Arctic, three-hundred block."

"Why?"

"To visit Martha."

"Martha?"

"Martha Wright. Remember, you asked about her after church?"

"One of the older ladies you were talking to?"

"Ah, ye of declining brain cells, you remember."

I'd turned left on East Arctic Avenue in front of the Tides Hotel.

"Now that we've determined the who, how about why?"

"Martha loves animals. I've never been there but have heard she has a bunch of pets. She puts food out every night for hungry, homeless critters. I was told that if you walked by her house around sunset, you could see animals of all sizes, shapes, and kinds. The Ark would've been too small to hold them all."

The purpose of our trip finally dawned on me. "You think Martha has Pluto?"

"It's possible. Martha's house is close to Dude's if you go as the crow flies, or as the Pluto trots. He didn't have a collar and he's adorable. He could've been tempted by the food and as friendly as he is, I can see Martha taking him in. I don't know why I didn't think of it before." He pointed to a large, two-story, new, sky-blue house on our right that backed up to the beach.

I said, "Looks like Martha can afford plenty of pet food."

"I hear she's worth millions. She plops a couple of C-notes in the collection basket each week. Her husband died a few years ago, and she moved here from Atlanta. Rumor is hubby hated the beach and wouldn't leave the Peachtree State. He didn't have to. Now he's planted there, and Martha has her beach. A best-of-both-worlds' marriage."

"What's your plan? Knock on the door and ask if she's stolen any dogs?"

"Doubt that'll work. I'll start with my charming smile, then step aside, and you can ask if she heisted the little fellow."

We climbed what seemed like a hundred steps to the front door, and Charles, good to his word, rang the bell, and moved back. It must've sounded like the dinner bell. There were barks ranging from high-pitched yelps that sounded more like squeaks, to Barry White rumbles. None of the noises sounded like someone answering the door. Charles rang again, again receiving a cacophony of animal utterances.

Charles leaned closer to the door and said, "Hear Pluto in there?"

I looked at him and shook my head.

"I don't either," he said. "Pluto's not a big talker, takes after Dude."

Still no answer.

The garage door was closed so we couldn't tell if a vehicle was inside. Charles suggested we walk around back and see if Martha was in the yard. The back yard consisted of a thirty-foot deep patch of perfectly mani-cured grass, before steps that led to the beach. There must have been two dozen stainless-steel bowls along the rear of the house, with half of them overflowing with dog food. It was no wonder that canines, and I suspected a few cats, racoons, and an occasional opossum chose this restaurant for their evening meal. What wasn't in back was Martha Wright.

"Now what?" I said.

"Other than breaking in?"

"That's not an option."

"You're right," Charles said and looked at the back door.

"Some of those dogs sound like they could have us for dessert."

That wasn't my reason for not committing a crime, but if it stopped Charles, I'd agree with him.

"Let's see if the neighbors know anything," he said, and looked to either side of Martha's house.

No one was in the yard, and for as far as we could see, the beach was deserted. We returned to the car and Charles looked across the street.

"Wonder if Dixie's home?" Charles said and started across the street.

Charles had already started up the steps of the house directly across from Martha's, so I assumed it was Dixie's. All I knew about her was that she attended First Light Church, and according to Charles was an uber-gardener and Martha's close friend.

We had better luck at Dixie's door. I recognized the woman who answered from church. She was in her late seventies, tall, at roughly five-foot-nine, thin, with hair so white that I suspected it might glow in the dark. Her face was tanned and leathery. She smiled at Charles and her teeth matched the color of her hair. She had on a white, long-sleeve men's dress shirt and jeans with mud caked on each knee.

"Charles, my oh my, what a pleasant surprise. Who's your friend?"

Charles nodded in my direction. "Dixie, this is my best friend, Chris Landrum. Chris, meet Dixie Thompson."

We exchanged pleasantries and Dixie invited us in, something I'm not sure I'd do if I found two guys who looked like us at the door.

"I wasn't expecting company, so things are a mess. I just came from the garden. Would either of you like a drink?"

"Water would be nice," Charles said.

She winked at me and said, "I've got bourbon."

"Water's fine," I said.

Charles and I sat on a burgundy sofa. Dixie was gone several minutes before returning with water in plastic glasses for Charles and me. She went back to the kitchen and returned carrying what I'd always heard referred to as a rocks glass filled with ice cubes and an amber-colored liquid. The odds on it being tea were slim. Her house wasn't nearly as new as Martha's and the living room furniture had been new in the 1950s. Dixie sat across from us in a white-on-khaki medallion patterned chair. She didn't seem worried that her muddy jeans would hurt it.

"Don't get me wrong, I love company, but what brings you gentlemen out today? Surely it's not to visit an old lady."

"Now Dixie," Charles said, "you're not old."

"Charles, you're a dear. You may not know this, but I pride myself in being able to spot bull dung a block away." She gave Charles a smile incongruous with her words.

Charles smiled. "You caught us, Dixie. We were at Martha's and it doesn't appear she's home. You know everything that goes on around here, so I figured you'd know where she is."

Martha smiled and wiggled her forefinger at Charles. "Did you forget what I said about my bull dung meter. I don't know everything, but I know Martha's whereabouts."

Charles smiled and said, "Where?"

"Dayton, Ohio. She's visiting a cousin who had a stroke."

I asked, "When's she coming back?"

"Christmas Eve, if the danged airlines don't mess up her flights. They're getting worse every day. You wouldn't catch me dead flying anywhere." She hesitated and bit her lower lip. "I do worry about Martha."

Charles asked, "Why?"

She frowned and shook her head. "The dear lady would slap me senseless if she knew I was telling you this. Her memory's slipping. She says she's fine, but she's fibbin'. If you ask me, she's on the road to Alzheimer's."

I said, "I'm sorry to hear it."

Charles jumped in with, "Who's taking care of her pets?"

"I offered to. She said don't be silly that it wasn't safe for me to be crossing the street to her house." She shook her head. "Charles, I've crossed that street for thirty-five years. Haven't been flattened yet. She hired a pet sitter; can you believe that? I'd never heard of such until Martha told me about it. The sitter, a sweet little thing, can't be over twenty, comes twice a day to feed and walk Martha's dogs. Didn't have jobs like that when I was a youngster. They sure didn't."

Charles said, "What time does the pet sitter come?"

"Lordy, young man. Do you think I sit here and keep tabs on what happens across the street? I have no idea when the sweet little thing shows up."

"Dixie," Charles said, "do you know if Martha took in any new pets in the last few days? Maybe an Australian Terrier?"

"Now that's one strange question, Charles. I don't have the vaguest idea." She took a sip, set her glass on the table beside her chair, and said, "You missing one?"

Charles told her about Dude and Pluto.

"Oh, dear. I can't imagine Martha stealing someone's pet. No, I can't. Don't get me wrong, my good friend loves, really loves, dogs and cats. I don't understand why she takes so fondly to them, but she does."

Charles leaned forward on the sofa. "Harry Truman once said, 'If you want a friend in Washington, get a dog.'"

Dixie looked at him like he sprouted a second head. "What's that have to do with Martha?"

Excellent question, I thought. "Charles likes to quote US presidents."

Charles glanced at me and back to Dixie. "It means that I understand how your friend can love dogs. Where did she get the ones she has over there?"

"Don't know about all of them. I know she's taken in strays over the years. One look at them and you can tell they were strays. Your friend's dog didn't look like a stray, did it?"

Dude looks like a stray and Pluto takes after his owner, so I wasn't ready to say no.

Charles didn't have my reservation and said, "Absolutely not."

"There you go," Dixie said.

"You're sure you don't know when the pet sitter will be back?" Charles said.

Her hand balled into a fist and she glared at Charles. "I told you I don't know."

She was getting annoyed, and I didn't blame her.

"Dixie, I hear you have one of the nicest gardens on Folly," I said to lower her level of irritation, or so I hoped.

A smile returned to her face. "I like to think so. Would you like to see it?"

Not really, I thought. "I'd love to."

She finished her liquid relaxer and led us through the kitchen to a deck, and down the steps. I knew as much about gardens as I did about the flora and fauna on Iceland but could tell that Dixie's was special. There were fifteen, four-foot-by-six-foot raised cedar rectangular boxes, each a foot high. Three rows of low shrubs and a row of ornamental grasses were behind the beds.

Dixie started telling us what each thing was and pointing out the name holders beside each item. Most of the flowers weren't in bloom, but it didn't stop her from telling us about them. It wasn't long before I zoned out when she was giving us the Latin name of the flowers and described the lasagna method of layering the mulch that works best for each variety of whatever those things were that were planted in each box. Charles, being Charles, was taking in everything the tour guide said. I started paying more attention, particularly where I was walking, when she mentioned having to occasionally "scat" a snake out of the garden. Dixie was in her element and her mood improved with each description, or it could have been heightened by the drink she had before giving us the tour. Charles wisely didn't ask her anything else about Martha or the pet sitter, and I fended interest until I'd reached my limit and said that we needed to be going.

"You can have another drink before you leave."

I said we'd love to, but I had somewhere I had to be. Charles continued to be wise by not asking me where. He wrote his phone number on a piece of paper he found in his back pocket and gave to Dixie and asked her to call if she learned anything about Pluto.

Chapter 17

Confucius said, "A ringing phone after midnight seldom brings glee." Okay, he didn't say it, but should have.

"Brother Chris, this is Preacher Burl. I apologize for waking you."

He knew me enough to know that if I wasn't asleep by ten o'clock, it was a bad night.

"That's okay," I lied. "What is it?"

"Something happened, and I wonder if I could inconvenience you to delay sleep and come over."

The clock read 12:15.

"Now?"

"The police just left and—"

That was all it took. I interrupted and told him I'd be there as soon as I got dressed.

Every light in Hope House was on as I pulled in the parking area. Shadows from the live oak beside the house snaked across the side of the parking lot, giving the house an ominous feel.

Burl was standing at the open front door waiting for me. His eyes were bloodshot and his shirttail untucked. "Please come in."

I followed him to the living room to find Bernard, Adrienne, Rebekah, and Joy seated on the sofa and two of the chairs. The Christmas lights were off and the presents under the tree looked forlorn.

Joy jumped up when she saw me and gave me a hug. She had on a heavy, brown bathrobe and was barefoot. "Thank you for coming. I asked Preacher Burl to call you. I was scared and feel close to you since you saved me."

"I'm glad he called. Is everyone okay? What happened?"

"Brother Chris, would you like something to drink? I have coffee brewing."

"I'm fine, Preacher."

Burl nodded and turned to Joy who'd returned to the sofa. "Sister Joy, would you like to start?"

"I don't know much," she said and pulled her knees up and wrapped her arms around them. "I was falling asleep, maybe already asleep. I heard a noise at my door like someone fiddling with the knob."

Burl added, "The knobs are old and make a lot of noise when they're turning. Sorry, Sister Joy, go on."

"Everyone here respects each other's privacy, so I was surprised that someone was trying to get in without knocking. I sat up and said, 'Who is it?' The noise stopped, and I heard what sounded like someone walking away."

"The old floors squeak a lot," Burl interrupted.

Joy continued, "I rushed to the door to see who was there." She turned to Bernard who was in the chair beside her. "I must've been loud when I asked who it was."

Bernard said, "You weren't that loud, Sister Joy. I was awake."

Burl said, "Bernard's room is beside Joy's."

"Preacher Burl," Bernard interrupted, "may I continue?"

"Of course."

"I heard Sister Joy and opened my door to see what was going on. The hall was dark, but I saw the outline of a guy rushing toward the steps. I started after him, and—"

Adrienne said, "Bernard nearly knocked me down. I stepped out of my room on the other side of Joy's to see what the commotion was about, and Bernard tried to run over me."

"Adrienne, I apologized. You came out so fast I didn't see you."

Adrienne pulled her robe tight and smiled. "Apology accepted."

I said, "Then what happened?"

Bernard looked at his fellow housemates to see who was going to interrupt him next. Everyone remained silent, so he continued, "After Adrienne tried to tackle me, I yelled for the intruder to stop. He didn't. I followed him down the stairs and out the back door. I was barefoot and not quite as fleet as I was in my younger days when I was traipsing around Afghanistan. The troublemaker was out of the yard in a flash. Gone, poof." He held out his hands, palms up. "That's about it."

"Brother Chris," Burl said, "I heard Brother Bernard yell and came out of my room to see what was going on. He told me about the outsider, so I called the police and asked the residents to join me in here.

Rebekah yawned and spoke for the first time. "I slept

through the whole thing. Preacher Burl woke me up and asked that I go to the living room. I have to be at work at six and was asleep before everyone else."

"Sister Rebekah, I'm sorry to have disturbed you."

"That's okay, Preacher. I was sharing so Chris would know where I was during it all."

"Did anyone get a clear look at the man?" I asked, again, to get the conversation back on track.

Burl said, "Brother Chris, I don't believe so."

"No, sir," Bernard added.

Joy and Adrienne shook their heads.

"I was asleep and didn't see anything," Rebekah said.

"Preacher," I said, "you once mentioned that you lock the exterior doors after everyone is in for the night. How'd he get in?"

"Brother Chris, the doors were locked, but as you can imagine, the locks are old and Officer Spencer, who responded to my call, said the back door looks like it was jimmied allowing access."

I remembered the first time I visited, a broken lock on the front door was being repaired. Burl tried to keep the house as secure as possible, but I could see how someone could get in without much trouble.

"Preacher why would someone want to break in?"

"I can only speculate. It should be obvious to everyone that there are no great riches here, no valuable jewelry, little cash. If a burglar sought to steal something of value, he would've been better off breaking in any other house on the island."

Bernard raised his hand.

Burl said, "Yes, Brother Bernard?"

"From my way of thinking, he was after Joy. He was

trying to get in her room. Someone took her before. Tied her up, put her on a boat, took her out in the ocean, and probably planned to throw her overboard. Yes sir, he was after her."

Burl said, "Now, Bernard, we don't know that."

"Preacher," Rebekah said, "can I go? I've got to get some sleep before my shift."

"Of course, Rebekah. Bernard, Adrienne, why don't you head upstairs and get some sleep."

The three of them slowly walked upstairs. Joy and Burl remained seated and watched the others go.

"Chris," Joy said, "I'm scared. I don't remember everything, but bits and pieces are coming back. That man was after me."

Burl moved beside Joy on the sofa and put his hand over her hand. "Sister Joy, go ahead and tell Brother Chris what you told me before you went to your room."

"I think I was a bartender, and that's why the bars over here looked familiar. I didn't work in those places, but watching their bartenders struck me as familiar."

"Do you know where you worked?"

"Not exactly. I remember it was smaller than the ones I've been in on Folly. Darker, too. I remember overhearing two guys talking. I wouldn't swear to it, but it seems like they were talking about a robbery."

"Like they were planning one or talking about one that'd already happened?" I asked.

"I'm not certain, I'm really not."

"Sister Joy, you told me that they didn't know you overheard what they were saying."

"Yes, Preacher, that's what I said." She looked at the floor and then at me. "What if I'm wrong?"

I nodded. "And they saw you and figured you were a threat."

"Then caught me, took me out to sea, and wanted to drown me."

I nodded. "Joy, can you remember anything else about where you worked, or about the two men?"

"The bar was dark, really dark. It's small. Most of its customers were dressed like they did physical labor. Muddy boots, yes, I remember several of them wearing muddy boots."

"Anything else?" I said.

"No, sorry. Chris, if that guy who broke in here was one of the men who took me, they know where I live. I'm scared."

"Sister Joy," Burl said, "I'm going to call Larry at Pewter Hardware as soon as it opens and have him install better locks on our doors. I should've done it long ago."

I hoped that would be enough.

Chapter 18

It was two in the morning before I got home, and another hour before I fell asleep. I don't normally watch the morning news, but it took all my energy to get out of bed after the early morning trip, so sitting in front of the television was all I had energy to do. I wasn't paying attention until the anchor mentioned an overnight break-in at Grogan's Fine Jewelry in Mt. Pleasant and threw the broadcast to a reporter standing in front of the store.

The reporter looked like he was ten years old pretending to be an adult dressed in his light-gray suit, red and green Christmas tie, and a white shirt that was loose around his neck. He was standing in front of the strip center that housed Grogan's. Yellow crime scene tape stretched across the front of the building and provided a visual loved by television cameras. The reporter held the mic in front of an older gentleman with curly white hair, wearing a black suit, a conservative burgundy and gray tie, and an expression that reminded me of an undertaker.

"Mr. Grogan," the reporter said, "how did the burglars get in? Also, can you tell us what was taken?"

"The lock on the back door was picked, and the thief somehow disarmed the alarm. Our most precious items were in the safe and undisturbed. Unfortunately, being three days before Christmas, our inventory was much larger than any other time of the year. Space was tight in the safe and we left several pieces in the display cases that weren't visible from the windows." Mr. Grogan smiled. "Many of our gentlemen customers wait until the last minute to shop for their wives or lady friends, so we're always prepared for the last-minute Christmas rush from procrastinators. As you know, we're known for our high-end jewelry and luxury watches."

"I must confess, I'm one of those procrastinators," the reporter said, and smiled. "One last question, Mr. Grogan. What would you estimate to be the worth of what was taken?"

"We've not had time to do a complete inventory, but I'd guess it was in the one-fifty to two-hundred-thousand-dollar range."

I patiently waited through three commercials to hear the weather. An unseasonable warm front was pushing throughout the area, and the temperatures were projected to soar into the lower seventies. Barb called while a sports reporter was raving about the good season the College of Charleston Cougars were having and his prediction about tonight's game against Coastal Carolina. I answered the phone and missed the prediction.

"Any news about Pluto?" she said, instead of hello. She had become acclimated to Folly phone etiquette.

"None that I've heard."

"Why not? What have you been doing all morning?"

She knew I normally would've been up for a couple of hours and I told her it was a long story and I'd tell her later. She said she was walking to the bookstore and if I wanted, she'd fix me a cup of coffee on the condition that I stop at Bert's and get her something for breakfast. I told her it was the best offer I'd had all day. She suggested that it was the only offer I'd had all day.

"Guilty as charged. I'll be there in a half hour."

Denise, one of the personable clerks, welcomed me with a smile and the question that I hear way too often. "Any word on Pluto?"

I told her no.

She said, "Poor Dude. I hope the pup comes home soon. I can't imagine how sad Christmas will be for him if Pluto's not there."

Denise went to wait on a customer, and I headed to the case where there were two cinnamon rolls begging for me to take them with me. I gave in to their wishes and headed to the cash register.

"It's about time you got here," Barb said, her smile indicating that she was kidding. "I'm starved."

We went to the office in the back of the store where she fixed two cups of coffee and I pulled two paper plates out of the drawer and adorned each with a cinnamon roll.

She looked at her watch. "I can't believe you've gone this long in the day without checking with Dude to see about Pluto. You're slipping."

I told her about my late-night call from Burl and what'd happened at Hope House.

"Do you think someone was there to harm Joy?"

"I don't know. The residents are convinced that's the case."

Barb sipped her coffee and set the mug on the glass-top table. "Speaking of Joy, let me tell you something that happened yesterday after work."

I took a bite of roll and nodded for her to continue.

"You know my vacationing neighbors."

"Troy and Nate," I said and figuratively patted myself on my back for remembering their names.

"Yes. I was in the elevator going to my condo, and before the door closed, Troy came around the corner and asked me to hold it open. He was pushing one of those big luggage carts. It was empty, and I teased him about having such a light load. He chuckled and said that they were checking out."

"Aren't they supposed to be here a couple more weeks?"

"They were. I asked if the weather was too hot for them. He laughed and said no that something came up and they had to leave early."

"That's unusual. All he said was something came up?"

Barb nodded. "I wouldn't have thought much of it until I remembered something, I believe it was Nate who said it the night before. We were in the parking lot talking about the weather, our usual conversation when we couldn't think of anything else to say. Nate asked how Joy was doing. It threw me a little until I remembered that he'd met her. I was vague and said as far as I knew, she's fine. Nate was silent for a few seconds and then asked if her memory was returning."

"Is that all he said?"

"I didn't want to answer yet didn't want to be rude. I said I didn't know. He didn't say anything else."

I watched her take a bite of roll, and said, "Are you thinking that they may be the men who took Joy?"

She swallowed and sipped her coffee before shrugging. "I have no reason to believe that they are. It simply struck me as strange that they were asking about someone they'd only met once, and that they were leaving two weeks early."

"Leaving early because Joy's memory might return, and she'd remember that they took her?"

"You said it, not me."

"You have good instincts about stuff like this. What's your gut tell you?"

Barb smiled. "Good instincts because I spent years defending white-collar crooks?"

I returned her smile. "Could be."

"Okay, here goes. My gut tells me that I don't know. Their actions struck me as strange."

"Strange enough for me to share with Chief LaMond?"

"You know her better than I do. What would she do with the information?"

"First, she'll give me a lecture about nosing in her business. Let's see, second, she'll repeat the lecture adding a few East Tennessee phrases that mean I'm a jackass." I paused and thought about previous times I'd shared none-of-my-business thoughts with Cindy.

Barb said, "Third?"

"She'll hang up on me or say something like, "'Okay, buttinsky, tell me again who these guys are, what they said about Joy, and when they checked out.'"

She took another sip of coffee, looked at my phone I'd set on her desk, and said, "What are you waiting for?"

Two rings later, Chief Cindy LaMond answered with, "This better be important. I have a meeting in five minutes with the mayor and rumor is that he's spittin' nails about how one of my brilliant officers shared his displeasure with a vacationer from Vermont about the speed in which he was traversing East Erie Avenue."

"I wouldn't want you to be late for your pleasant conversation with His Honor. Call me when you get a chance."

I told Barb that by hanging up on me, the chief meant that she'd love to call me.

Neither of us believed it.

Chapter 19

One thing I've learned over the years is if I'm walking on
Center Street, there's a good chance I'll see someone I
know. The appropriately named street is only five blocks
long, yet most all of the island's restaurants and retail estab-
lishments are either on it or within a block.

Since the weather was picture-perfect, I left Barb's books
and turned right and ran into Cal, more accurately, he ran
into me. He was walking with his head down and humming
"White Christmas." I put my hand out to keep him from
stepping on my foot.

"Oh, sorry. Guess I was daydreaming." He tipped his
Stetson in my direction.

"Are you ready for your party?"

"Yes, umm, no, well maybe."

"Glad you clarified that," I said and smiled at the
crooner.

"That's where my mind was wandering when I plum

near ran you down. Trying to figure out what else I need to do."

"While I'm thinking of it, I talked to Joy, and she's planning on being there."

"How's her memory?"

"A few are coming back."

"She know who she is, other than Joy?"

"Not yet."

"I remember how screwed up I was after getting conked on my noggin. It's harder for her." He shook his head. "Not even knowing any of the who, what, where, and whys of her life."

"True."

Cal said, "Heard more about Pluto?"

"I haven't talked to Dude today, so I don't know if the pup's still missing."

"That'll be a mighty big Christmas double-downer. No memory and no Pluto."

I agreed and told him that if he needed help to get ready for his party to give me a call.

"Much obliged, pard."

He tipped his Stetson again and moseyed on.

I walked two more blocks to the Folly River Park, the site of several oversized Christmas decorations and the official city Christmas tree. The lights were on, but the cloudless day made it difficult to appreciate the illuminated displays. Regardless, there were two young mothers holding toddlers and pointing to the outline of Santa's sleigh and then at the tree.

At the edge of the park a foot pier crossed a portion of marsh and jutted over the Folly River. Leaning on the wood railing at the far end of the pier was a familiar, bright red

University of Arizona Wildcats sweatshirt wrapped around Charles Fowler. He appeared in deep-thought as he stared at the water and didn't notice me walking toward him until I was within a few yards.

"Hi, Chris. Nice day, isn't it?"

I said, "What's wrong?"

"Why think something's wrong?"

I shrugged. "*Hi, Chris. Nice day.* Charles, that's something a normal person would say."

He shook his head and returned to gazing at the water. "Sorry I didn't insult you."

I stood close to him and waited for him to continue.

We watched several cars cross the bridge to the island and Charles finally said, "It seems that this year's been mired in deep manure. Poor Heather was thrown in jail and accused of killing her manager and then tried to kill herself. Now she's gone." He continued to stare at the slow-moving water.

Charles and Heather had dated a few years. She was a country music singer and had convinced Charles to move to Nashville with her at the urging of an unscrupulous manager who took her hard-earned money along with her hopes of a singing career. They returned to Folly six months ago with Heather's dream crushed. She left the island, and left Charles a farewell note, hours before he'd planned to propose marriage.

I was tempted to say that everything would be okay. Not knowing if it would be, I didn't say anything.

Several minutes passed before he said, "Now add to Heather leaving, poor Joy doesn't know who she is, and may be in danger. And, that's not even mentioning Dude missing his best buddy." He looked at me. "Chris, this is a seriously sucky year, and Christmas is almost here."

I remained silent.

He finally said, "Know where I was for two hours this morning?"

"Malibu," I said. An absurd answer to a question I couldn't know the answer to, usually got a smile from my friend. Not this December 22.

"No," he said, expressionless.

"Where?"

"Sitting outside Martha Wright's house."

"Waiting for the dog sitter?"

He nodded.

"Did she show up?"

He shook his head and said, "Guess."

"No."

"No, you're not going to guess? No, you think she didn't show up, or no to Pluto being there?"

I should have stuck with Malibu.

"Did she show up?"

"No."

"Sorry. Want to go back?"

"Thought you'd never ask."

He'd walked to the River Park, so I suggested we go to my house and take my car.

We ran into Bernard in front of Mr. John's Beach Store.

"Y'all looking for Pluto?" he asked to begin the conversation.

I told him we were and asked if that's what he was doing.

"Yes, sir. Dude woke Preacher Burl and me up when he pounded on the door as soon as the sun stuck its head over the ocean. Scared the shi… umm, crap out of me until I saw it was Dude. He said Pluto was still AWOL and wanted to know how long it'd be before we started looking."

Charles said, "What'd you tell him?"

Bernard smiled. "Well, I bit my tongue, so I wouldn't say I hadn't planned on looking. The poor little hippie looked so sad. I told him I'd be out as soon as I got dressed." He pointed to his jacket and slacks. "And, here I am."

I said, "I know Dude appreciates it."

Bernard started to leave, turned, and said, "Chris, have you talked to Joy this morning?"

"No, why?"

"I was heading out and only saw her a second. She's going to call to tell you she remembered something that could be important."

"Thanks, Bernard. I'll give her a call."

He gave me a quick salute and headed in the other direction.

Charles moved to the edge of the sidewalk, leaned against the fence in front of Mr. John's, and pointed to the pocket that held my phone.

Message received. I started to call Hope House.

He grabbed my hand. "Wait. Got a better idea. We need to go see her. That way, both of us can help her remember."

I didn't know if a visit would help her remember better, but the best way to improve Charles's mood was to give him a purpose.

"Good idea."

A block from Hope House, Charles yelled for me to pull over. I pulled between a rusting motorhome and a pile of broken tree limbs. Charles was out of the car before I put it in park. I waited to see where he was going before I opened the door. I didn't have to go far. Charles jogged between two houses and was returning before I saw what had drawn his attention.

He said, "Thought I saw him."

I waited for his findings.

"It was a little dog the same color as Pluto." He pointed between the two houses. "The guy back there was calling Lulu." Charles sighed. "Not Pluto."

I said, "Sorry," and followed my dejected friend to the car.

"Thought for sure it was him," Charles mumbled.

He appeared sadder now than he'd been when I found him on the walking pier. I pulled in Burl's parking area and was afraid Charles was going to stay in the car. I was beginning to agree with him that this year was mired in deep manure.

Chapter 20

Preacher Burl waved us in. He said Joy and Adrienne were in the living room watching television. Joy smiled when she saw us, and Adrienne looked like she would have been as well off if we weren't there. Burl asked if we wanted coffee. I told him that would be nice, and Charles showed as much enthusiasm as Adrienne had shown seeing us.

"Joy," I said, "Bernard said you had something to tell me."

Burl returned and handed us mugs of steaming hot coffee. He asked the ladies if they wanted more. They declined, and Burl returned to the kitchen to refill his mug.

Joy watched me take a sip, and said, "Yes, but you didn't have to come over. I was going to call."

I told her we were in the area and thought it would be better to stop.

"Thank you. Don't know if this means anything. I woke up around one remembering being in a little apartment. It had a green blanket on the bed and a kitchen so tiny that the table was up against the wall and there was barely room to walk past it. Funny that I would remember those things."

"Were you there with the man from the boat?" Charles asked, showing more life than he had all morning.

She closed her eyes and turned her head from side to side. "I don't think so. I had the impression it's where I lived."

Charles said, "Remember anything else?"

"The whole place was small, not much more than a bedroom, a kitchen, and a bathroom."

I said, "Were there windows?"

Her eyes widened. "I didn't think of it until you asked. I don't remember one in the bedroom, just the ugly green blanket. There was a window over the kitchen sink."

I leaned closer. "Good, you're doing great. Let's say you're standing at the sink. Can you see anything out the window?"

She closed her eyes again. "Not really—no, wait, there's a gravel drive between my building and a long, narrow brick building. There's a *No Parking* sign on the building."

"Is that all?" interrupted Charles, who has the patience of a puppy.

"I think so."

I said, "Joy, let's try one more thing. Is there a door leading outside from the kitchen?"

"Chris, I can't remember." She lowered her head and repeated, "I can't remember."

"That's okay, Sister Joy," Burl said. "You're doing good, isn't she, Chris?"

"Yes, Joy, you are."

Adrienne appeared bored with our conversation and stared at the television. I glanced up to see what was so fascinating and saw a newscaster with a photo of the jewelry store on the monitor behind her. She was talking about the burglary that I'd seen reported on the earlier newscast.

Burl looked at the screen. "Why is it that such a glorious Christian holiday brings out the worst in people?"

"Preacher," Adrienne said, "places get broken in all the time. I don't think it has anything to do with Christmas."

"I suppose you're right, Sister Adrienne. It's just that—"

Joy interrupted, "Turn up the sound."

Joy's tone startled Adrienne. She dropped the remote, uttered a profanity, apologized to Burl, and grabbed the device off the floor.

All of us were now staring at the television. The story concluded with the newscaster telling her viewers to call the police if they knew anything about the burglary. An auto dealership ad promoting it's *gigantic Christmas sale* blared from the screen. Adrienne muted the sound, and Joy continued to stare at the silent screen, and Charles asked who buys someone a car for Christmas?

I waved for him to stop talking and turned to Joy. "What are you thinking, Joy?"

She turned away from the television, glanced at Preacher Burl, and then at me. "Chris," she said, no more than a whisper. "The bar was dark. I had to get a case of beer out of the storeroom. Budweiser. The sound system, actually it wasn't more than a cheap, grease-covered CD player, was blasting a Bob Segar song." She hesitated and looked at the floor. "Two men at the end of the bar were huddled together, and…"

"And what?" Charles asked.

She looked at him, looked back at the floor, and gazed at the television. "I don't know."

"Joy," I said, "why did that jewelry store burglary remind you of being in a bar?"

"I'm not certain. It must've had to do with the men."

"That's good, Joy," I said. "Two men were huddled together. Did you hear something they were saying?"

She glanced back at the television like it would miraculously give her the answer. "Seger's 'Old Time Rock-and-Roll' was playing. Was loud. Then it stopped." She jerked her head in my direction. "I heard one of the guys say the name of that store that was on TV."

"Grogan's Fine Jewelry," Charles said.

Joy continued to look at me, and said, "Yes."

I nodded. "Joy, I know this is hard. Why don't you close your eyes and try to remember back? You were in a bar, a dark bar. You went to get a case of beer, so do you think that's where you worked?"

She didn't answer but nodded.

"Okay, good. The two men were talking but you couldn't hear them because of the loud music."

She nodded again.

"The music stopped, and you heard one of the men say Grogan's Fine Jewelry."

"Said Grogan's, don't think he said the rest of the name."

"Okay, good. Did you get a good look at the men?" She closed her eyes. Charles started to speak. I put my forefinger to my lips. He remained silent.

"Chris, I'm sorry. No. They faced the other direction. It was dark, so dark."

"You don't remember anything else they said?"

She shook her head.

"Joy," Charles said, "did the men see you listening?"

Good question, I thought.

Burl leaned forward and nearly fell out of the chair. He caught his balance, and said, "Do you think they thought Sister Joy heard them planning to rob the jewelry store?"

Charles tilted his head to the side. "Yes."

"And took her so she couldn't tell anyone?" Burl said.

"There's a good chance that's what happened," I added.

Adrienne finally stopped looking at the television and twisted around on the sofa toward us. "Joy," she said, "do you remember the name of the bar?"

An even better question.

"No," Joy said. She returned to looking at the floor. Her left hand balled in a fist, her right hand trembled.

"Joy," I said. "You've done great. I know this is rough. Why don't we stop pestering you and let you rest?"

Charles glared at me.

Burl stood and said, "Sister Joy, let me get you more coffee."

"Thank you, Preacher," she whispered.

"Brother Chris, Brother Charles, would you like more?"

"No thanks, Preacher Burl, we need to be going."

Charles continued to glare at me. He wasn't ready to leave.

"Brother Burl," Adrienne said, "do you think we, umm, Joy is safe here? What if they come after her again?"

"Sister Adrienne, the man from Pewter Hardware is coming this afternoon to put on the new locks."

"What about the locks to our rooms—to Joy's door?"

Burl smiled. "All the doors will get new locks."

"Thank you, Preacher Burl," Joy said, and made a valiant effort to smile.

"Joy," I said, "Is it okay if I tell the Chief what you shared?"

"If it'll help."

"It will, thanks. Please call if you remember anything else."

Charles and I stood to leave, and Joy jumped up and gave each of us a hug. Adrienne surprised me when she moved behind Joy and when Joy stepped back, she stepped forward and hugged Charles and me, and whispered, "Thank you for caring."

Chapter 21

"Why'd you want to hightail it out of there?" Charles groused as soon as we were in the car. "Joy was figuring out what happened."

"She was struggling. She couldn't remember anything else. I was afraid it'd hurt more than help if we pushed her, besides, she said she'd call if she remembered more."

He sighed. "She's close to remembering what happened. The quicker she does, the safer she'll be. You don't really think new locks will keep them safe, do you? The burglars broke into a jewelry store. That store's locks had to be better than whatever Larry installs, and the store had a security system."

Charles had a good point. Regardless, Joy will remember when she remembers. We can't push her. I was going to share that morsel of wisdom with him when the phone rang.

"Okay," Cindy LaMond said, "what was so all-fired important for you to call?"

"Hello, Chief, how was the meeting with the mayor?"

Charles was flailing his arm around to get me to put the phone on speaker. I did, and he gave a thumb's up.

"The bad news is despite the best efforts of one of my officers to get me fired, I'm still chief."

I pulled in the drive of a house that appeared vacant, so I could focus on the call instead of driving.

Charles leaned closer to the phone, and said, "What's the good news?"

"Chris, you got a Charles stuck in your throat?"

"Got a Charles stuck in my car," I said.

"Poor boy," Cindy said.

I assumed she meant me instead of Charles.

Not to be deterred, Charles said, "The good news?"

"I'm still getting a paycheck and get to drive around in a nifty vehicle with a siren and I don't have to pay for it."

"Congratulations," Charles said.

"Enough about my wonderful life. Why'd you call?"

I told her what Barb had said about the Canadians checking out of their condo two weeks early.

"Holy moly Chris, you know how many people check out early from rentals, hotels, condos, and tree houses?"

"How many?" Charles butted in.

"First, Charles, I asked Chris, not you. Second, I don't have a flippin' clue. It's got to be several. Things happen that we didn't count on. Plans change."

"True," I said. "There's more. Barb also said the guys were asking if Joy's memory was returning."

"I want to know that myself. So what?"

"So, they're two men from outside the area with no reason to care about Joy or her memory. I know it's a weak link, but don't you find it interesting that they're interested in her memory, and then leave Folly when her memory starts returning?"

"Weak link," Cindy said, "It's a feeble, puny, scrawny link, and that's giving it too much credit."

"I know. Regardless, Barb said she had an uneasy feeling when the guys were talking about Joy."

I heard Cindy sigh. "Suppose it's better than no link. Barb didn't happen to know what the guys drove, their license plate number, or their home addresses, did she?"

"No. She said they rented through Avocet. I suspect a police chief who still has a job and a vehicle with a siren could wrangle that information out of the rental agency."

"Okay, I'll do it for Barb. We chicks need to stick together. Anything else you want to share while you have my less than undivided attention?"

"Yes," Charles said, "we just—"

"Charles, I was talking to Chris."

"In fact, yes," I said. I told her about our visit to Hope House and Joy's vague memories of an apartment, most likely hers, and seeing two men in the bar and their mention of the jewelry store that was burglarized. She stopped me and said she needed to get something to write on. I heard her rustling papers, and she asked me to repeat everything.

I did, and Charles added, "Larry's going to replace the locks at Hope House this afternoon."

"That I knew," she said. "That's the advantage of sleeping with a hardware store owner."

"Ewe," Charles said.

"Chris, and I mean Chris, did Joy happen to remember the name of the bar or the location of the apartment?"

"Afraid not."

"Anything else, *Chris*."

143

"No, sorry."

Charles said, "That's it, Chief."

Charles pointed at the next cross street. "Next stop, Martha Wright's house."

I turned right and back toward town, so I could get on East Arctic Avenue, the one-way street headed toward Martha's. Her drive was empty.

"Crap," Charles said. "How can the danged pet sitter sit if she's never here?"

Add that to the lengthy list of questions to which I had no answer. I pulled in the drive and didn't know if Charles thought the pet sitter walked to the house or someone dropped her off. He bounded up the steps and rang the bell and received the same response that he'd received the last time he tried. Barks in several octaves reverberated through the house, and the door remained closed. We headed to the back yard where we found more of the bowls had food in them then during our last visit. Someone had been here.

Charles shook his head, and said, "Want to wait for the sitter to come back?"

"That could be hours."

"Or minutes," he said, with more optimism than I could muster.

"I don't think it'll do any good to wait. Besides, we don't know that Pluto is still missing."

Charles pulled his phone out his pocket and tapped in a number. "Yo, Dude. This is Charles. Is—" His head bobbed from side to side. "Oh." The head bobbed some more. "I'll keep looking."

He ended the call. "Pluto still 'be bye-bye.'"

"Sorry."

"Me too. Why don't you go on home? I want to stay and wait for the sitter. I'll walk home."

"You sure?"

He said he was, and I left him on Martha's front steps.

I took an extra-long route home in the unlikely event I'd see Pluto hitching a ride, and to think through what Joy had said about an apartment and overhearing two men talking about the jewelry store that happened to be burglarized overnight. I couldn't shake the fear that she was in danger and that I couldn't do anything to lessen that chance.

Chapter 22

I awoke early the next morning and realized that I hadn't had anything substantial for supper. I checked the weather on my phone and saw that it was already in the low-fifties; a glance out the window revealed that it was sunny. A walk to the Dog would be good for me even if French toast wouldn't.

I stepped through the entry and was greeted by Amber.

"Merry Christmas Eve, Eve," she said and pointed to my favorite table, which was empty and waiting for me.

I thanked her for holding the table for me.

"You're not that important," she said with a smile. "Nobody else wanted it."

With my ego sufficiently deflated, I slid in the booth and she said coffee and water would arrive shortly. I thanked her and looked around the near-empty restaurant. Marc Salmon was at his usual table near the center of the room. He nodded in my direction and said he was waiting for

Houston. I smiled and nodded, acknowledging his comment.

Amber returned with my water, a cup of coffee, and a question. "Has Pluto returned?"

I told her I didn't know, but as of yesterday afternoon, he hadn't.

"Nope," Marc said from the center of the room. "I saw Dude on my way here. He was looking for his little buddy."

"That's too bad," Amber said. "Hope the little fellow's okay."

"And, hope Pluto is too," Marc teased.

Amber and I smiled but didn't comment on the councilmember's joke.

Bernard stuck his head in the door and headed my way.

"Would it be possible for me to join you?"

"Sure," I said, like I had a choice with him standing in front of the table eying the seat across from me.

"Thanks, Broth—umm, I mean, Chris. Sorry, sir, Preacher Burl's got me talking like that." He sat and unbuttoned his faded army jacket.

"Chris, do you know what the word mistletoe means?"

That was a question I'd never been asked. "No, what?"

"Get this," he said and smiled. "It's derived from two old-time words that mean poop on a stick. Can you believe that?"

"You made that up."

"No, sir. Saw it on TV this morning. It seems that mistletoe seeds are eaten by birds, and then pooped on tree branches, and the seeds grow into mistletoe. Ain't that a hoot?"

Now there was a Christmas story I hadn't heard before, and doubt Preacher Burl had ever shared from the pulpit.

"Bernard, that's interesting. Do me a favor and don't tell Charles."

"Poop on a stick is safe with me," he said. "Knew you'd be interested."

He didn't know me as well as he thought he did. "What brings you out so early?"

"Thought I'd walk around a while and look for Pluto. Besides, the kitchen was getting a little too uncomfortable for my liking. Joy, Rebekah, and Adrienne were gathered around drinking coffee and complaining about men. I felt like I was the enemy, being of the male species."

I was tempted to laugh, but saw that Bernard was serious. "What were they saying?"

"Not exactly sure. I walked in on the conversation. Joy was saying something about men and escaping off the boat. Adrienne was saying that they knew what Joy was talking about and that she was at the house after being deserted by an abusive husband who left her for his massage therapist. I didn't hear Rebekah's problem with guys, but from the look on her face, it must've been bad."

Burl had shared the information about Adrienne, but I didn't know anything about Rebekah other than she worked at Black Magic. I was curious about Joy and asked Bernard if she'd said anything more about being on the boat since she'd been unclear about what had happened when she talked to me.

Before he answered, Amber was at the table asking what we wanted to eat. I said French toast. Amber acted shocked.

Bernard said, "That sounds mighty good, ma'am. I'll try some."

Amber smiled and said she thought she'd be able to find him French toast.

She left, and Bernard said, "Nice lady."

I agreed, and he asked what my question was again. I asked if he remembered anything new that Joy had said.

"Not that I heard, other than she was on the boat and was tied up by two men."

"She said two men?"

"Yes, sir. I remember because it was the first time I'd heard her talking about being on the boat. It got my attention because there was only one guy who tried to break in her room. Why?"

"She'd only mentioned one man when she talked to me."

Bernard scratched his head. "Wait, there's something else. Some of us were talking last night about how we got around on Folly. Rebekah and I don't have wheels and hoof it. Adrienne has an old Chevy pickup truck. Smokes like a pile of damp logs on a fire. Joy said she didn't have a car or a truck and had to walk from her apartment to work."

That was new, and I asked him if she knew where her apartment was.

"No, sir. All she said was that she had to walk."

"She say anything else?"

"Nothing she hadn't said before."

"How well do you think she's adjusting to Hope House?"

"Better than I'd be doing if I didn't have a memory and didn't know why someone took me on a boat to do whatever they planned to do. I can't see how it could've been anything good. It's fortunate that she managed to slip out of the ropes that were on her ankles and wrists. She said the next thing she remembered was how the storm was flinging water over the bow and how the guys in front were fighting to keep it from overturning. Then she was in the water, clinging to a surfboard."

Some of that was news to me. "Did she tell you that or are you guessing about what happened?"

"She said it last night, sir. I couldn't have thought that up on my own."

Our breakfast arrived, and Bernard stuffed three bites in his mouth like he hadn't eaten in days.

He took another bite and pointed his fork at me. "Got a question for you, Chris. We live in a big place, the biggest house on the street, with lots of bedrooms. How do you think the man trying to break in Joy's room knew what room was hers? I'm thinking that someone living there must've told him."

"Any idea who?"

"It wasn't me, and I'd wager it wasn't Preacher Burl." He chuckled. "I don't have anything to wager, but you get my drift."

"I understand. What about the others?"

"That only leaves Rebekah and Adrienne. I know Adrienne better than I know Rebekah. She doesn't strike me as someone who would do something bad like that. She's a loner so I don't know who she could tell. Rebekah, come to think of it, has been seeing someone, or that's what she says. None of us have seen him."

"What do you know about him?"

"Near nothing. It's someone she met at Black Magic."

"Customer or employee?"

"Sir, that's more intel than I have access to."

"How do Joy and Rebekah get along?"

"I haven't seen them conversing much. The most I'd ever seen them talking was on Woody's Wednesday."

"Woody's Wednesday?"

"Burl picks up two large pizzas from Woody's each Wednesday. I think he pays for them some weeks and other times they're donated. Other restaurants occasionally kick us a few meals, but Wednesdays are my favorite."

"That's nice of the restaurants."

"Preacher has made a lot of friends since opening First Light. It makes us feel like we're part of the community."

"Back to Joy and Rebekah. Do you remember them saying anything about what happened to Joy?"

"Nah. It was more girly stuff, you know, like makeup, hair, and how stupid men are."

"Nothing else about the men who took Joy?"

"No, more than anything, I think we're all nervous about somebody sneaking around the house and talk to each other to keep our minds off it. We'll rest easier after the hardware store man gets the locks changed. Hope he doesn't charge too much. Money's in short supply. If it wasn't for the donated food, I don't know what Preacher would do."

"I know Larry LaMond, the man who owns the hardware store. He'll give Preacher Burl a good deal."

Bernard nodded. "Good. Money don't grow on trees, you know."

"Bernard, you said you thought it may've been someone living there who told the intruder which room was Joy's."

"Yes."

"What about someone who used to live there?"

"Chris, there've been a bunch of people since I moved in. I don't remember some of them. How could we figure out which one?"

"Most of them wouldn't know which room was Joy's. What about people who recently moved?"

"If they moved before Joy moved in, how would they know which room was hers?"

"Process of elimination."

"Chris, you're going to have to dumb that down for me."

"They'd know which room you, Adrienne, and Rebekah were in, and where Preacher Burl lives. They'd know that Joy was in one of the other rooms."

"Got it. Let's see, there's Al. No, he moved a few weeks before Adrienne moved in. Besides, he moved to California. Scratch him." He took another bite of breakfast and rubbed his chin. "Okay, in the last couple of weeks before Joy arrived, two guys left. There's Alex and Taylor."

"Tell me about them."

"Let's see, Taylor left after Preacher Burl found him a job in North Charleston. Lucky man. And, there's Alex Rockford. Never did trust him and was glad to see him go."

"Where'd he go?"

"Don't know. He was there for supper one evening and gone by the time breakfast was served. I don't like spreading rumors, but I heard he'd been in jail for burglary. Don't know if it's true."

"When did he leave?"

"Give me a minute. Oh yeah, it was the day the faucet in one of the bathrooms broke and water spewed all over the room. Had to get a plumber. I'll tell you, it was a mess."

"Bernard, when?"

"Oh, two days before Joy showed up."

"Would Taylor and Alex have known which rooms would've been vacant when Joy moved in?"

"I would think they'd know that their rooms would be empty."

"Anyone else?"

"Not that I recall."

Bernard took the last bite of breakfast, wiped his mouth with a napkin, and said, "Chris, I sure appreciate you letting me break bread with you." He smiled. "Preacher Burl says break bread a lot. It's rubbing off on me."

I returned his smile and said, "Worse things could rub off on you."

"One more thing. Could I impose on you to lend me a few dollars to cover my breakfast. My inheritance hasn't come through yet, and you wouldn't believe how difficult it is to pull money out of a stock portfolio."

I smiled and told him I'd take care of the breakfast. "Under one condition," I added, "you call me if you hear Joy say anything new about her ordeal."

He saluted, said, "Deal, sir," and left the restaurant with a full stomach and a smile.

I had nowhere else to be, and the Dog had several vacant tables, so I asked Amber for more coffee. She returned with the coffee and asked if I'd run Bernard off with my boring conversation. I told her no, and that I reserved boring conversations for Charles since he doesn't listen to anything I say.

She patted me on the arm and said, "Don't be too hard on yourself, I'm certain that in the decade you've known him, he must've heard something you said."

I thanked her for the vote of confidence, and she smiled and headed to a table in the center of the room to spread more holiday cheer.

I took a sip of the refreshed mug of coffee and tried to recall everything Bernard said that Joy shared, especially anything new.

Joy seemed more certain that there were two men on the boat instead of only one as she previously mentioned. Also, one of the things that I couldn't previously figure out was how she'd untied herself, grabbed a surfboard, and got off the eighteen-foot-long boat without the men knowing. I hadn't thought about how horrific the storm had been the day before we found her. If the men were struggling to keep the boat from capsizing, it was possible that she could've slipped overboard before they noticed her missing. They probably figured she drowned with the storm so intense, which was probably their intent from the beginning.

Joy also told Bernard and the others that she didn't own a vehicle and that she walked from her apartment to the bar where she worked. It could've been a bar on Folly since they are all within easy walking distance of most buildings with apartments, yet, her description of the bar didn't fit any that I was aware of.

Then, what about Bernard's theory that one of the current residents told the man who was trying to get in Joy's door which one was hers? Even if he was right, how could anyone prove it. Even if you add residents who recently moved, you have the same problem.

I left the Dog with a full stomach, a lighter wallet, and more unanswered questions than I had entered with. At least, I knew the origin of the word mistletoe.

Chapter 23

It was turning out to be one of the warmest late-December days I could remember, so I headed to the far end of the Folly Pier to walk off a few of the hundreds, okay, thousands, of calories I'd devoured with my French toast. The Pier, like much of downtown Folly two days before Christmas, was nearly deserted. A handful of diners were enjoying an early lunch in Pier 101, but there couldn't have been more than ten people strolling along the thousand-plus-foot-long fishing pier. From the end of the structure, I had a view of much of the island's Atlantic shoreline and in the distance a glimpse of the county park where I first met Joy. With a little imagination, I pictured the area of the ocean where she bailed from the boat. It was a miracle that the surfboard carried her to safety.

The phone rang as I was climbing the steps to the second level of the Pier.

"Mr. Landrum, this is Joyce, I mean Joy."

I asked how she was doing.

"Okay. I just saw Bernard, and he said he had breakfast with you. Are you still at the Lost Dog Cafe?"

I told her no, where I was, and asked why.

"I remembered a few more things overnight, and you told me to let you know so you could tell the police. I could call them but feel more comfortable talking to you."

"Want me to come by the house?"

"I'd like to get out of here. If you're going to be there for a while, I could walk over and meet you."

Thirty minutes later, I saw her heading my way. I waved from the upper deck and she smiled and returned my wave. Her hair was pulled in a neat ponytail and she had on jeans, a white blouse, and a gray jacket.

She said, "Thanks for waiting."

I motioned for her to join me on the bench. I didn't tell her I had nowhere else to be.

She looked toward shore, and said, "This is my second time out here. It's relaxing."

I agreed and waited for her to get to the reason for the visit. If the walk to the end of the pier relaxed her, I'd hate to see her when she wasn't. Her hand moved from her lap to pushing an errant strand of hair behind her ear, back to her lap, and then zipped and unzipped her jacket.

"Joy, are you okay?"

She continued to look at the hotel, and said, "How would I know if I'm okay? I don't know who I am, where I should be, who I should be with, and what'll happen next."

I understood that, yet she appeared more anxious than the last two times I'd been with her. "I don't know how I'd handle it either."

She slowly turned my direction. "Have you heard of a bar called something like Blackbeard's?"

"I don't think so. Why?"

"It came to me during the night. It may be where I worked."

"Have you asked anyone else?"

"No. I'm not sure who I can trust. I know I'm being paranoid, but the guy trying to get in my door freaked me out. I think I can trust you."

I told her she could. I also knew that anyone could say that and saying it didn't make it true.

"Joy, is that all you remembered?"

"I don't think I worked there long."

"Why do you say that?"

"It didn't seem that familiar, like I couldn't find the clean bar towels. I know it sounds silly, and I could've remembered it wrong. It's vague."

I took out my phone and searched for Blackbeard's Bar in the Charleston area. There were numerous references to the notorious pirate called Blackbeard, most of them talked about his terrorizing merchant ships along the coast in the early 1700s. There were nearly as many pirate tales in the Lowcountry as there were ghost stories, and those were in the too-many-to-count range. There was only one bar with Blackbeard in the name.

"Joy, does Blackbeard's Hangout Bar sound familiar?"

"Vaguely. Is that a bar over here?"

I showed her a photo of the front of the bar from its website. "Look familiar?"

"I'd love to say yes. Honestly, I can't tell. Where is it?"

"About seven miles up Folly Road. Would you like to go there?"

She jerked her head in my direction. "When?"

"We could go now."

"Like, right now?"

"Now or later today. It's up to you."

"I don't think ... okay. Would you mind?"

"Gosh, Joy, it'll take valuable time away from me sitting here wasting the day away."

She smiled. "I might learn who I am." She closed her eyes and was silent for the longest time. Finally, she said, "Let's go before I chicken out."

We were leaving my drive ten minutes later. I didn't tell Joy, but I started to question what we might face. What if she worked at the bar and someone there was the person who'd abducted her? We pulled off the island, and I wondered if I should've asked Charles to go. What if we're headed into danger?

Joy didn't help when she said, "I'm scared. I want to know who I am, yet, what if I don't like me?" She turned in the seat and faced me. "What if the men who took me are there? I might not know who they are."

I'd driven this stretch of Folly Road numerous times, in fact, one of my favorite restaurants, the Charleston Crab House, was less than a half-mile from Blackbeard's Hangout Bar, yet I couldn't recall ever seeing our destination. When the street numbers indicated we were there, I understood my confusion. There was a deteriorating strip center on the left and at the far end of it was a narrow storefront with a faded-black awning and the words Blackbeard's Hangout Bar in Old English script. If I hadn't been looking for it, I wouldn't have noticed the sign. Several cars were parked at the other end of the shopping center in front of a dollar store and a nail salon. No vehicles were in front of the bar and the plate-glass windows were painted black, so I couldn't tell if anyone was behind them.

"Joy, does anything look familiar?" I said and parked in front of the black awning.

She stared at the door, gripped the center console, and whispered, "That's where I work, where I worked."

Joy's paranoia was rubbing off on me and I thought the smart thing for me to do was to call Cindy LaMond and see if she could "visit" the venue with us. We were out of her jurisdiction, but I would've felt safer visiting with someone carrying a weapon.

"Let's get this over," Joy said before I could make the call.

"Are you sure?"

She nodded and opened the door.

For better or worse, here we go.

Chapter 24

Compared to Blackbeard's Hangout Bar, the darkest bar I'd ever been in looked as bright as a polar bear in a snowstorm. We stepped into the darkness to the blaring sounds of "Dark Necessities" by the Red Hot Chili Peppers. There was a dim, red light over the exit door at the rear of the building, and I thought I saw movement from the right side of the room.

The song ended and someone with a deep, gruff voice said, "Well, look what the cat dragged in."

Whoever it was must have been wearing night-vision goggles or was a bat with a bass voice. I couldn't see anyone. Joy walked in the direction of the sound. I followed and hoped I wouldn't trip over a chair, table, or vampire.

"Kevin's going to have a cow when he sees you," said the voice. "You sure you want to be here?"

A refrigerator door opened, and its light illuminated the face of the man who pulled it open, and the person, I assumed, who'd been talking. I wasn't old enough by a couple of hundred years to have seen Blackbeard, but imagined the man standing in front of us shared a striking resemblance. He was at least six-foot-five, weighed two-seventy, with black, stringy hair that reached his shoulders and a beard that reached low on his chest.

My eyes were beginning to adjust to the near darkness, and I glanced around. The room was empty except for Joy, Mr. Blackbeard, and me.

"Do I know you?" Joy said to the unsmiling bartender.

"Crap, kiddo, did you crack your skull and forget the only friend you had here?"

He wasn't far off.

She smiled. "Something like that. What's your name?"

"You're serious, ain't you?"

I stepped closer to the man dressed in black. He could've been one of those creepy creatures in a Halloween haunted house.

"Hi, I'm Chris. My friend Joy's suffering from amnesia. Did she work here?"

"Joy," the man said. "You mean Joyce?"

"Yes, and you are?"

"I'm Darryl. Joyce and I worked two shifts together, and then she disappeared. Thought Kevin was going to blow a gasket when she didn't show her next shift." He turned to Joy. "What happened, sweetie?"

"I don't know. Who's Kevin?"

Darryl waved his hand around the room. "Kevin Beard, owner of this dump."

With no music playing, I heard traffic on Folly Road, and a door slamming in back of the building.

Following closely behind the slamming door, came a higher-pitched voice that said, "Joyce Tolliver, if you think you're going to slink in here and get a check for the two days you worked, you're out of your freakin' gourd."

I stepped between the new voice and Joy. "Hi, I'm Chris Landrum, a friend of Joyce. Are you Kevin Beard?"

The room was still dark, but I thought I saw him nod.

"Is there somewhere the three of us can talk?" I asked and looked around for an office, hopefully with lights.

He headed to the far side of the room, and I followed. Darryl whispered to Joy, "Good luck. He's pissed."

Kevin ushered us into a small office that doubled as a storeroom. I thought Darryl's beard was long until I saw Kevin's. If it didn't reach his belt, it didn't lack much. He wore black slacks, black tennis shoes, and a white T-shirt. Cases of beer were stacked six high on one side, and three cases of liquor were on the floor beside two chairs with rips in their vinyl seats. They'd probably been taken out of service from the bar. Kevin pointed to the chairs, and we sat. He had a chair behind the makeshift desk but sat on the edge of the desk.

"What happened, Joyce? I thought you were going to be reliable. You gave me a song and dance about how you never missed work and had bartending experience. You said you lived in walking distance, so you could be here whenever I needed you."

"Mr. Beard, Joy, umm, Joyce, had a traumatic event that caused amnesia. She—"

"Mister, was I talking to you? I asked Joyce a question. What are you anyway, her doctor?"

"Mister Beard, Chris is a friend who saved my life. He's right about my amnesia so we'd appreciate it if you could tell us what you know about me."

"Joyce, I told you when I hired you to call me Kevin. You serious about losing your memory?"

"Yes. How long did I work here?"

"Two nights. A Friday and Saturday. You were scheduled to be off Sunday and come in Monday. The last I saw you was when you left that Saturday."

"They've shown my photo on television. Didn't you see me there?"

"Joyce, guess you don't remember me telling you this when you hired on. This is probably the only bar in Charleston without televisions. My customers are here to grab a drink and don't want to be caught up in sports and politics, stuff that dominates the danged TV. I don't even have a television in my house, although it wouldn't matter, I'm never there. This place is my life."

"Kevin," I said, and hoped he would allow me in the conversation. "Joyce really has amnesia. What can you tell us about her?"

He glared at me and I was afraid he wasn't going to say anything, at least nothing pleasant. He slid off the desk, moved behind it, opened a drawer, and pulled out a manila folder that had scribbling on the front and a tab that was peeling off the top. I couldn't read what was on the paper he pulled out of the folder, but it looked like a job application.

He looked at the document and up at Joyce. "Your application says that you're Joyce E. Tolliver, age forty-seven. Born in Kansas City, Kansas, and ain't got any living relatives." He looked down at the paper and flipped it over to the other side. "Any of this coming back to you?"

She shook her head.

"You have a management degree from Kansas State

University. It's not on the application, but you told me that you'd been married to an eye doctor, an optometrist. Something about him leaving you for one of his patients." Darryl smiled, something I didn't think was in his repertoire. "I remember why you told me someone with a job in management wanted to tend bar. Said you were bored working in an office and took part-time bartending jobs." He glanced at me and turned to Joy. "You remember any of this?"

"Afraid not, Kevin. Did I tell you what brought me to Charleston?"

"Nothing other than you said you moved around a lot. Spent time in Texas, Oklahoma, and I think Georgia. That's all you said."

"Were you here the second night she worked?"

"I'm here every Saturday night. I done told you that's the last time I saw her."

"Do you remember if there was a crowd?"

"Good, but not one of my best. Why?"

I didn't want to tell him too much about what'd happened. For all I knew, he could've been one of the abductors. "Just curious. Something may have happened to Joyce after she left here."

"Like what?"

"We're not certain."

"Joyce, you remember telling me how you walked home after work and I said I'd get you a ride if you wanted? It's not good having an attractive lady like you walking around at two in the morning."

"I don't remember that."

"Sorry," he said. "Of course, you don't."

"Kevin, do you remember Joyce talking to a couple of men more than others that night?"

"Chris, that's your name, right?"

I nodded.

"You saw how dark it was out there. If my hands weren't connected, I'd have trouble knowing where they were most of the time."

I assumed that meant no. "Didn't you wonder what happened to Joyce when she didn't return?"

"Sure. She didn't have a phone, so I couldn't call. Besides, she's not the first person I hired who skipped out after a few days. This isn't the most fun work, and I struggle to get good help. Getting any help. I figured you'd moved on to another job or skipped town."

"Kevin, this may sound like a strange question, where does it say I live?"

He was looking down at the application and slowly raised his head and looked at her. "You really don't remember anything?"

"No."

"Wow," he said and shook his head. He gave her the name of the apartment complex off the application. He told her it was three blocks behind the bar and that it'd been there forever. I asked if an apartment number was listed. He glanced at the application and wrinkled his nose. "Nope. Wonder why I didn't catch that?"

"What about the other paperwork you need on a new employee," I said.

He glanced over at Joy and returned his gaze to me. "I was desperate to fill the bartender's job. The last one walked out on me with the weekend around the corner. Joyce said she had bartending experience. That was enough for me. I told her that we would get all that done the next week when things slowed down."

He looked at her again. "You didn't come back to do it."

He was getting either nervous about not filling out the required paperwork, or angry that we were pestering him. We thanked him for the information and stood to leave.

"Joyce, if you get your memory back and want to come back to work, I could find a place for you. Sorry about whatever happened."

Kevin stood in the office's doorway as we weaved our way through the dark room.

I nearly bumped into Darryl who was standing by the front door. He gave Joy a hug and said he was sorry she wasn't still working there. She thanked him, and he glanced back at his boss who was still standing in his office doorway. Joy opened the front door and Darryl slipped me a folded piece of paper, patted me on the back, and said, "Take good care of Joyce. She's a nice lady."

We left on much better terms than when we'd arrived, as Coldplay filled the air with "A Sky Full of Stars."

I didn't know if I should look at the paper in front of Joy, so I slipped it in my pocket and headed to the car.

Joy stopped me. "Can we walk to where I lived, umm, live?"

"Do you remember the way?"

"Not really. Didn't Darryl say it was three blocks that way?" She pointed behind the bar.

We walked three blocks in the direction Darryl had indicated and found two apartment buildings. They were decades from being new and backed up to each other with a gravel alley separating the structures. There were no signs listing the name of the complex or anything indicating there was an office. The apartment numbers were the same style, so I assumed they were part of the same development. *Now what*, I wondered. "Anything look familiar?"

Joy looked at the building on our side of the alley and then at the one on the other side. "Not really."

I jotted the street name and address on a card from my pocket and said that I'd call Chief LaMond and see if she could find out anything about the apartments and the company that managed them, and with luck, which apartment had been rented by Joyce Tolliver. She agreed and said she'd like to get back to people she knew.

Joy was exhausted by the time I pulled into her parking area. She had her hand on the car's door handle. Instead of getting out she said, "The rain was blowing sideways. Ocean water lapped over the side of the boat and my head kept bouncing off the wooden arm rest each time we hit a wave. I was soaked, and I twisted my arms until the rope I was tied with loosened enough for me to pull my hand free." She closed her eyes, gave an abbreviated nod, and continued, "The man in the seat in front of me cussed the weather and kept saying the boat was going to sink. I managed to untie my feet and grabbed the surfboard and slipped over the side. I didn't know where we were but knew the farther away from the boat I could get, the safer I'd be." She stared at the house and then said. "Chris, the next thing I remember was you and Barb looking down at me on the beach."

Chapter 25

I returned home, poured a glass of Cabernet, and plopped down in the living room. I would have bet money on Charles's reaction to my trip to Joy's former place of employment and would've won.

"You did what?" he blurted before I got to the part about meeting the Blackbeard lookalike.

"Charles, why don't you let me finish and you'll know what I did."

"You wouldn't have to tell me if you'd let me go," he said, in a voice that would make a sniveling, ten-year-old, with hurt feelings, throwing a tantrum sound like Gandhi.

I continued sharing what we learned at Blackbeard's Hangout Bar, and from the unsuccessful visit to the apartment complex Joy listed on her employment application.

"Joyce Tolliver, Joyce Tolliver. I like Joy Doe better. How did she take it?"

"As well as you can imagine. I was going to call Cindy

and tell her but wanted to call you first." I hoped to get a glimmer of appreciation from him.

"You wouldn't have had to call me at all if you'd taken me with you."

"Are you finished reminding me?"

"Not sure. What happens now?"

"I end this cheerful discussion and call Cindy."

"You could've already called her. You wouldn't have had to call me if you'd taken me."

I did what some of my friends had done to me on more than one occasion. I hung up on him.

The next call also went off the tracks before I got it headed in the direction I'd desired.

"Glad you called," Cindy said instead of hello, reinforcing my dislike of caller ID. "Let me tell you about our two friends from north of the border."

"The Canadians?"

Cindy made an audible sigh. "No, Santa and Mrs. Claus."

I smiled and asked what she'd learned.

"I got a call this afternoon from Staff Sergeant Major Urton from the Royal Canadian Mounted Police. I'm a lowly ole cop in this humble burg, so I haven't the foggiest how high or low a staff sergeant major is in the RCMP pecking order, but he seemed nice, although a bit stuffy when I asked if he rode a horse to work and wore a red coat and one of those funny wide-brimmed hats."

"Cindy, what'd he say?"

"Patience, Charles in waiting. He was reporting on what he'd learned about Troy Ellis and Nate Cook's early departure from our slice of heaven. It seems that Nate's mother was in an auto accident near Ottawa. A lumber truck driver decided that one of those pesky stop signs wasn't applicable to him and poor Mrs. Cook made the mistake of being in the intersection at the time. She's in critical condition, and Nate's father called and asked him to come home."

"You don't think he had anything to do with Joy's abduction?"

"Unlikely. There goes your number one and number two suspect. Any other brilliant ideas?"

It wasn't brilliant, but I reminded her that I was the one who initiated the call, and shared what Joy and I'd learned from our trip to Joy's former place of employment. Cindy scolded me for not letting her know where we were going. She added that I was too old, or in her words, "Way too fossilized to be gallivanting around where angels fear to tread." I reminded her that Joy and I had simply visited a bar where she may've been employed and not barging in on a gang of thieves, abductors, and other mischief-makers.

"How'd you know that before you got there?"

She was right although I wasn't going to give her the satisfaction of agreeing. I asked if she could use her official resources to learn about the apartment complex where Joy allegedly lived and find the landlord to get a key to her apartment.

"Chris, you know I'm at your beck and call, whatever that means, and live and breathe to seek answers to your countless questions."

She then did what I did moments earlier to Charles. The phone went dead.

It was two more sips of wine before I remembered the note that Darryl had handed me.

It read: *Call me. I know the guys you asked Kevin about.* He added a phone number.

I punched in the numbers and four rings later was afraid no one was going to answer. Finally, I heard a rock song in the background that I didn't recognize, and a voice that I did. "Yeah."

"Darryl, this is Chris, the guy with Joyce earlier today."

"Listen, I can't talk now. Can I call you at this number in about an hour?"

I said he could.

The next hour lasted about a week, or so it seemed, until the phone rang, and Darryl said, "This Chris?"

I said it was.

"Listen, I'm on a break and can't talk long. I overheard you talking to Kevin. It's amazing what you can hear in here when the music's not vibrating the walls. You asked about two guys who Joyce was talking to during her last shift. Kevin's protective of his customers and flat-out lied when he said he didn't know anything about it. He says many customers have been hassled by cops. He wants this to be a, how does he put it? Oh yeah, a hassle-free zone."

That was way more than I wanted to know. "Darryl, the guys?"

"Yeah, them. Listen, I've seen them in here a few times, didn't know them well. I don't know what their deal was, but the last two times they talked all hush-hush like. Looking around like they were planning to overthrow the govern-ment and not wanting anyone to hear."

"Did you ever hear what they were talking about?"

"No, but I think Joyce did."

"Why do you say that?"

"The last day she was here, I was getting off shift and

grabbing my coat from the back room. Joyce was with me and started to go behind the bar near where the two guys were sitting. She stopped in the doorway for a long time. I couldn't tell what she was doing. I headed out and didn't think anything else of it until I heard you talking to Kevin. I figured it could've been important and had something to do with Joyce losing her memory. Am I right?"

"I think so. Did Joyce say anything to you about it?"

"No. I waved bye when I left and didn't say another word to her until she showed up today."

"Do you know who the guys are?"

"Only their first names. Raymond and Taylor."

"Know anything else about them?"

"Raymond's fond of Miller High Life; Taylor's a Bud guy. That's it. Sorry."

"What do they look like?"

"White dudes. Looked like most of our other customers. Jeans, casual clothes. Average height. Raymond's a couple of inches taller than Taylor. Not fat, not thin."

"Age?"

"I'd guess late thirties, could be off several years. I'm not good with ages."

"Have you seen them since that night?"

"I was off a couple of days. They weren't in after that while I was here."

"Anything else?"

"Not that I remember. You really think they had something to do with what happened to Joyce?"

"There's a good chance. I'm going to have to let the police know what you've said, so you might get a visit from someone from Folly Beach or the county sheriff's office."

"I'm not a fan of cops. There's a history there." After a

long pause, he sighed. "If it can help Joyce, I'll talk to them. She seems like a nice lady."

"She is. I appreciate you telling me about the men."

"No problem," he ended, with one of my least favorite sayings.

Chapter 26

I've known a few Raymonds. Taylor was a more unusual and memorable name, and if I'm right, was the name of one of Burl's recent residents. A phone call to the preacher should verify it.

"Ah, Brother Chris, it's good to hear from you," he said, although he hadn't heard anything from me yet, and was responding to my name appearing on his phone.

"Good evening, Preacher. I hope I'm not interrupting anything."

"In fact, you are. We're having a Christmas party. Why don't you hop on your sled and have the reindeer bring you over and join us? Sister Joy was getting ready to tell me about your afternoon adventure. I know she'd love for you to be here."

I remembered how down she was when she got out of the car after our visit to Blackbeard's, but I also knew it was a Hope House party and didn't want to butt in. I thanked

Burl for the invitation and shared my reluctance to crash the party.

"Nonsense. You wouldn't be crashing, I invited you. Besides, Sister Joy was saying how much she enjoyed spending time with you, and Brother Bernard was recounting how you and Charles had invited him to last year's party at Cal's. Remember how you encouraged him to speak with me about being homeless and the tough time he'd had finding a homeless shelter? It meant the world to him. He'd like to see you."

I wasn't keen on the idea of going out again. I was more reluctant to turn down a generous offer from a minister this close to Christmas. Besides, I wanted to ask him about Taylor. I said I'd head over.

The seasonal lights around the front door and along the roofline were in full holiday splendor. The house looked in much better repair in the dark than during daylight. Bernard greeted me wearing a stop-light red shirt and black jeans. He also greeted me with a smile, a firm handshake, and, "Welcome to the first annual Hope House Christmas party." He leaned close and whispered. "Alcohol's prohibited. Thought I'd warn you."

I thanked him for the welcome and the warning. He pointed to the living room where from the sounds of multiple voices I assumed everyone was gathered. Burl was standing on a two-step ladder by the tree and fiddling with a strand of lights that weren't working and Rebekah was putting a CD in a portable player on the table in another corner. Adrienne was sitting in the chair farthest from the action and looking either tired or bored.

Joy saw me in the doorway and jumped up from the sofa and rushed over and gave me a robust hug. She looked more refreshed than when I let her off earlier today but wore the same clothes.

"Preacher said you were coming. It's nice of you to join us."

Burl saw me and thanked me for coming while he was holding the unlit lights. He had on a red sweatshirt with a reindeer on the front, gray slacks, red house slippers, and a Santa hat. I asked if there was anything I could do to help, and he said he knew what the problem was and would soon have the lights burning brightly. He asked Bernard if he would take me to the kitchen to get something to eat and drink.

Elvis's version of "Santa Claus is Back in Town" began playing from the CD player and Bernard told me the drink menu included soft drinks and a fruit punch that he whispered was yucky. I selected Diet Coke before Bernard showed me the platter of peanut-butter sandwiches cut in half, and another platter of sliced celery, carrots, and for a reason I wouldn't attempt to guess, dried okra. Apparently, Bernard couldn't guess either. He shrugged.

I filled a paper plate with portions of everything except okra and followed Bernard back to the party.

Elvis was singing "White Christmas," Burl had managed to get the lights working and was sitting on the sofa between Joy and Rebekah, and Adrienne was still in her chair expressionless. Bernard motioned me to sit in the remaining chair and lowered himself to a sitting position on the floor. I felt bad taking his seat, but not bad enough to stand and try to balance my food and drink while eating.

"Here Comes Santa Claus," started playing and Burl said, "*Elvis' Christmas Album*. My favorite."

I knew who it was since at one time I had the same

album. Adrienne didn't appear to share Burl's appreciation for the King. She rolled her eyes.

Joy said, "I was getting ready to tell Preacher Burl about our trip to the bar when you called."

"That can wait," Burl said. "Wouldn't want to spoil the party. Chris, this is my first Christmas in here. I've been blessed this year."

Bernard said, "And we're blessed you chose to share the house with us, Preacher."

Rebekah added, "Bernard's right. We are blessed, Preacher."

Adrienne remained silent.

Joy didn't say anything. She was staring at the tree and I couldn't imagine what must be going through her mind. For me, Christmas has always been a time of reflection. It's been a time to look back, think about Christmases past, Christmases with family and friends, and while most people take New Year's Eve and Day to think about the future, I found it more meaningful to focus those thoughts at Christmas. Joy can't see back much more than a week. And, without that perspective, she wouldn't be able to see, predict, or even hope for things to come. I looked over and gave her a smile, hopefully received as one of love, trust, and hope.

She returned the smile, and Burl stood and said, "Brother Chris, we were getting ready to sing some Christmas carols. Now that you're here, we can add another voice to our group. Sister Rebekah, would you ask Elvis to take a break until we get finished caroling?"

Burl knew from listening to me in church that I had a terrible singing voice, so he clearly must be under the influence of Coke, the cola kind.

"That's okay, Preacher. I'd rather listen to your outstanding voices."

I had no idea how outstanding the others would be. All I knew was that compared to me, Alvin and the Chipmunks sounded operatic.

"As you wish, Brother Chris. It's not actually a carol, but let's begin with 'A Holly Jolly Christmas,' a ditty made famous by Burl Ives, a man named after me." The preacher chuckled at his joke; a joke that I was probably the only person in the room to catch. Preacher Burl was named after the singer Burl Ives because his father was a fan of the singing actor.

Burl raised his arms like he was going to direct a choir and began singing, "Have a holly, jolly Christmas; it's the best time of the year."

Few would argue with that sentiment. Many could argue that the sounds of this group singing couldn't make this the best time of the evening. That didn't stop the enthusiastic choir director from smiling and bouncing on the balls of his feet as he led the vocally challenged group through the song. Burl was the only person who knew the words past the first three lines, so he increased his volume to cover up the random words the remainder of the group were spewing. The sounds were sad, the intent uplifting.

The song came to a merciful end and Burl beamed like he'd been conducting the Mormon Tabernacle Choir. "Joyous," he said.

Not the word I would have chosen; regardless, the group was having an enjoyable time. Even Adrienne smiled.

"Great start," Burl continued. "Brother Bernard, what's your favorite Christmas carol?"

Bernard turned and looked behind him like it was

another Bernard the preacher was talking to. He then glanced at the Christmas tree and said, "Preacher Burl, I must say I've never given that much thought. I'll go with 'Away in a Manger.'"

"Then let's give it a go. Folks, let's make a joyful noise unto the Lord." He returned to his conducting stance and sang, "Away in a manger, no crib for His bed. The little…"

It may have been my imagination, but the singing sounded nearly on key. I mouthed the words and enjoyed the fellowship. After Bernard's favorite finished, the preacher asked Rebekah the same question, and she didn't hesitate when she said, "O Holy Night." We—they—muddled through it, when Burl turned to Adrienne and repeated his question.

"Preacher Burl, if I had to choose one, it'd be 'Pretty Paper.'"

Burl smiled and didn't tell her that the Willie Nelson penned song wasn't a carol. "Good choice," he said, and the group began singing Adrienne's selection.

It was heartwarming to see how not only the preacher, but everyone, embraced Adrienne's song. I also wondered what he would say to the newcomer who had no memory of the past. Would he ask about her favorite carol, or would he acknowledge her lack of memory?

We finished Willie's "carol," and Burl said, "Wonderful job."

I glanced at Joy who was staring at the floor like she was wishing to be somewhere else. I empathized with her.

Burl moved closer to Joy and said, "Sister Joy, instead of asking you about your favorite carol, let me say that when I look at you, I can't help but think about the beautiful carol

'Joy to the World.' Would you mind if I chose it as your song?"

Joy smiled and nodded.

That level of sensitivity was one more reason Preacher Burl was a godsend to Folly Beach and its residents without traditional church homes.

Burl returned to his role of conductor and led the group in Joy's song. With the final "And wonders of His love," Burl put his arm around Joy and said, "Thank you for being with us."

She mumbled, "You're welcome," and Burl turned to me. "Now Brother Chris, I don't have to ask your favorite. Last Christmas you told me it was 'Silent Night.' Folks, shall we sing the marvelous hymn to the man who's been pretending to sing with us?"

They did, and I was touched.

"I don't know about you," Burl said, "my throat is parched. Shall we take a break and refresh our drinks?"

No one protested and everyone except Burl and I moved to the kitchen.

Burl watched everyone leave, and said, "It wasn't lost on me that you called for a reason. Care to share it while the others are imbibing?"

"Preacher, didn't you have a resident named Taylor?"

Burl nodded. "That wasn't a question I'd anticipated. Yes. You saw him the day I was in the Lost Dog Cafe. Remember, I told you I was looking for someone about a job."

"I remember, although I didn't catch his name."

"He's Taylor Strong. He moved out the night before we were blessed by the appearance of Joy. Why?"

"Preacher, what can you tell me about him?"

"I assume you will answer my question at the appropriate time."

I nodded.

"Brother Taylor was only here a few weeks. He was quiet, not as quiet as Sister Adrienne, but quieter than the rest. He shared that he was originally from North Carolina, never said what town. Getting him to talk was a challenge. I managed to get that he'd had various jobs over the years. He said he'd been an armored car driver, and a clerk in a convenience store. He also shared that a few years ago he went to school to learn how to be a locksmith. In fact, the day you saw me looking for him, I was there to tell him about a vacant position in a locksmith company in North Charleston."

"Did he get the job?"

"He didn't tell me directly, but I gathered that he did and would be earning enough to move."

"You don't know for certain?"

"No." The preacher smiled. "It was fortunate that he left because that freed up the best room in the house for Joy."

Bernard and Rebekah returned and moved back to their previous locations. Adrienne came back and asked if she could get Burl and me something else to drink. The caroling must have put her in a better, if not more generous, mood. Burl said that another Coke would be great, and I said I'd go with her to get the drinks.

"Brother Chris," Adrienne said as she poured the Preacher's Coke, "this is one of the nicest nights I can remember. I love it here."

I was surprised since she looked bored most of the evening. Once again, I was reminded not to judge others by appearances.

We returned, and Burl led us in a few more Christmas songs, more secular than religious, and I told him I needed to be going. He walked me to the door.

"Preacher, would you do me a favor?"

"If I can."

"Call the locksmith shop and see if Taylor took the job?"

"I'll try, but tomorrow is Christmas Eve. I don't know if it'll be open."

I said I understood and asked him to try.

"You think he was one of the men who abducted Joy?"

I nodded.

"I pray not," he said.

"I'll be calling Chief LaMond in the morning. She'll probably be contacting you to learn everything you know about him. Do you know what kind of car he drives?"

"I'm horrible with stuff like that. I know it's a few years old and black. I doubt that helps."

We shook hands, and he told me to have a pleasant rest of the evening.

Chapter 27

Christmas Eve began as another beautiful day. The sun rose over the ocean a little after seven and was escorted on its upward path by wispy cirrus clouds. The temperature was already in the low forties, ten degrees above average. I decided that this would be a good morning to walk to the Lost Dog Cafe for breakfast. It appeared that I wasn't the only person to have that thought. Amber saw me enter and pointed to the only two empty tables. I chose the smaller of the two, and she had a mug of coffee in front of me before I'd wiggled out of my jacket.

"Merry Christmas Eve," she said and followed up by leaning over and hugging me around the neck.

"And the same to you. What are you and Jason doing tomorrow?"

She glanced around the room to see if her services were needed elsewhere. They weren't, and she turned back to me. "We're going to First Light's service and then to Samuel and Jacob's house for lunch."

Samuel was a good friend of Amber's son, Jason. Jacob, Samuel's dad, and Amber had been dating a year. Their first date was last Christmas at Burl's Christmas Eve service.

"Great. Is Jacob fixing lunch?"

Amber chuckled. "Jacob's a guy; Samuel's a guy. The best they can muster is burning toast. I'll do everything."

Jacob and Samuel's culinary skills had me beat, but I didn't remind Amber of my shortcomings. "It's great you'll get a chance to be together."

"I think so. Changing the subject, have you heard anything about Pluto? Dude was in for lunch yesterday and I thought he was going to cry when I asked him if his pup had turned up."

"I haven't heard anything."

"Don't know what'd happen to Dude if something happened to his short look-alike."

"I agree."

"Any news about Joy?"

Amber had earned her reputation of knowing all the gossip worth repeating.

I told her about going to Burl's party and how well Joy appeared to be adjusting to her new home. I then added, "Do you know Taylor Strong?"

"Name's not familiar. Why?"

I shared what Joy and I'd learned about her job at Blackbeard's and overhearing something that possibly resulted in her abduction.

"Want me to ask around?"

"Yes, if you limit it to people you can trust. I don't want Taylor hearing about it."

"Have you told the police any of this?"

"Some of it. I need to talk to Chief LaMond."

She pointed at me and frowned. "Yes, you do."

She took my order and headed to the kitchen.

My phone rang while I was waiting for food to arrive. I didn't recognize the number and nearly didn't answer. There are only so many "free" vacations I can win, or "opportunities" I must learn about the latest-greatest Medicare supplemental insurance.

"Chris, Chris Landrum," said the voice on the other end. It was familiar, but I couldn't place it.

"Yes."

"Oh good. This is Bernard, you know, the one at Hope House."

"Sure, Bernard. How are you?" I said, although I was more wanting to know why he was calling rather than how he was.

"I'm fine, sir. I was talking to Preacher Burl after you left last night. He told me you were asking about Taylor Strong. The preacher said you asked what Taylor drove, and Preacher didn't know. He's mighty good about knowing the scriptures; he's short on knowledge about some things in this here world. Cars are one of them."

"Do you know what Taylor drives?"

"Yes, sir. A black, 2013 Ford Focus. Got itself a dent in the front bumper. The rear tires have too much mileage on them and are nearly bald."

"Thanks. That may help the police find him."

"There's more, sir. It has South Carolina plates; the first three numbers are 339. I hate to say, I don't recall the last three."

"How do you know that?"

"That's the kind of unimportant stuff I remember."

"Bernard, that'll be helpful. It's not unimportant. Do

you know anything else about Taylor, other than he was a locksmith and moved out the night before Joy arrived?"

"I don't know the best way to put it, but he acted like he was in a box and no one could find a way in. Don't get me wrong, he was friendly enough. It's like he had secrets and didn't want anyone to get close enough to figure them out. Does that make sense?"

"Yes. Do you know if he had friends on Folly other than people in Hope House? Anyone ever come to visit him or to pick him up?"

"It wasn't at the house. I saw him on West Ashley talking to a man. They were huddled up against the wall at St. James Gate, near the opening to the outdoor patio. Know where I mean?"

I told him I did.

"I couldn't tell what they were talking about because I was on the sidewalk at the stoplight. It looked sort of sketchy, sir."

"Can you describe the other man?"

"Not really. He looked taller than Taylor and heavier. Sorry, that's the best I can do."

"That's fine, Bernard. Anything else?"

"Nothing about anything I know about Taylor. I know Preacher Burl tried to call the locksmith where Taylor was supposed to go to work. I think the place is closed until after Christmas. He left a message on the machine. I won't take up more of your time. Will I see you at tonight's service?"

I said I'd be there.

"Then, *adios*, sir."

Amber had slid my breakfast in front of me while I was talking to Bernard. I was on my second bite when Chief

LaMond came in the restaurant, looked around, and headed to my table.

"Merry Christmas Eve, Cindy. Care to join me?"

"You buying?"

"Wouldn't that be bribing a law-enforcement official?"

"Not unless you plan to ask me to do something illegal, immoral, or considering the season, un-Christian."

"None of the above. Have a seat."

Amber must have figured that the Chief would be joining me. She had a mug of coffee for Cindy before she had time to remove her jacket, and said, "Something to eat, Chief?"

"Anything expensive and put it on his tab." Needless to say, she pointed at me.

Cindy took a sip of coffee, and I said, "Dude find Pluto?"

She shook her head.

"Too bad. You working or taking today off?"

"What do you think? Dear sweet hubby's chained to the cash register at the hardware store and won't get home until every Tom, Dick, and Harriet buy every battery, extension cord, and those cheap, chintzy, *hecho en Mexico* Christmas ornaments that hang on the tree, spin, and play 'Jingle Bells.'"

"Sorry."

"I'm not. That's what makes him enough money to spoil me and allows me to live like a queen."

"A queen?"

"Whoops, I drifted into my fantasy world for a moment. Enough about my phantasmagorias life. Yes, I'm working. In fact, I'm waiting for a call from the landlord at the apartment where Joy lives, or where the owner of that bar thinks she lives. What other trouble have you been sticking your nose in?"

Cindy's expensive breakfast arrived, and I told her what Bernard had shared. She jotted down the vehicle information and said she'd see what she could find out, although she wasn't optimistic since, in her words, without the last three numbers of the license, there were "three billion combinations." I was certain that was a tad high but didn't get in an argument about math. I'd exhausted my latest information, and our conversation drifted to what she was doing Christmas Day—attending Cal's party, going to Planet Follywood's annual Christmas pot-luck dinner later in the day, and acting like a queen. I shared my plans.

I waited for her to finish eating, paid the tab, and walked with her to the door. In a moment totally out of character, she hugged me and said, "Merry Christmas, and thanks for being such a good friend."

She slid back to her normal self when she said, "You tell anyone I did that, and I'll have you arrested for embarrassing a public official."

I told her that the act of kindness was safe with me.

Chapter 28

I was headed home after leaving the Dog when the phone rang again. This time, I knew who it was.

"Merry Christmas Eve, Charles."

"Yeah, yeah. Where are you?"

"In front of City Hall."

"Park your butt on the nearest bench. I'll pick you up in ten minutes."

"Where are we going?" I asked, wasting words since he'd already hung up.

It couldn't have been more than five minutes before Charles' Toyota pulled to the curb and he waved me in.

"Could you tell me where we're going?" I asked, thinking it was not too much to ask.

He turned left on East Arctic Avenue, and said, "Dixie called and said Martha was home."

"Your plan is to barge in on Martha on Christmas Eve?"

"Nope. Figured you'd ring the doorbell and flash your old-man charm. How could she resist inviting us in?"

I could think of several ways and rolled my eyes.

I rang the doorbell and the sounds of her menagerie filled the house. Unlike our earlier visit, the door opened, and Martha said, "Hold on a second, Teri, I'll get your … Whoa, you're not Teri."

Charles stepped in front of me. "Hi, Martha, I'm Charles from church. This is my friend, Chris."

Martha wore gray sweatshirt and sweatpants. She leaned on her cane and looked from Charles to me. "Where's Teri?"

Charles looked down the steps and toward the street. "Who's Teri?"

"The child watching my family while I was away. She's supposed to stop by this morning to get her money." She stepped on the porch, closed the door, probably to keep her herd of family members inside, and looked up and down the street. "If you're not Teri, why are you here?"

"Chris and I stopped by the other day to see you. Your neighbor, Dixie, said you were out of town."

"Yes, I was up in Dayton visiting, poor Tommy. He had a stroke, you know. Got back last night. Flight was three hours late. Can you believe that?"

Charles said that he could.

"Oh, I'm being inconsiderate. Would you like a cup of coffee?" She hesitated and winked at Charles. "Or a hot toddy? I've got some good whiskey to spike it with."

Charles said, "Coffee would be fine."

"Give me a minute to herd my family into another room. Otherwise they'd lick the livin' tar out of you."

She opened the door enough to slip back in the house and Charles turned to me and whispered, "Wonder how long it'll be before we're begging for the hot toddy?"

The animals quieted to a low roar, and Martha opened the door and invited us in and led us to what she referred to as the "sitting room." I would've called it an animal play house. In one corner there was a three-foot-high, triple deck, carpeted cat tower. Beside the tower was a large wicker basket filled with rubber balls, a tennis ball that looked like it'd rolled under a running lawnmower, and a hard-rubber thing shaped like a five-pound weight. Other toys were located on the brown pile carpet.

She told us to sit anywhere we liked while she got the coffee and asked again if we were sure we didn't want a toddy. I declined, although I was getting closer to saying yes. We each chose one of the three wingback chairs and lowered our bodies in the dog and cat hair infested seats. I noticed an end table beside my chair holding a large aquarium. It wasn't more than a foot away, so I saw there was no water in it. What it was filled with was a boa constructor that was a mile long, or so it seemed. It stared at me and I knew what a mouse must feel like on its way to supper—the boa's supper.

Martha returned to the room carrying two, white china cups of coffee. "Oh," she said, "I see you've met Squeezy. Would you like to hold him?"

Where was the hot toddy when I needed it? "That's okay, Martha. Not today." *Not tomorrow, not ever*, I thought.

"Martha," Charles said, "You have a lovely house."

"Thank you. It's comfortable, and wonderful for my pets."

Charles asked, "How many pets do you have?"

"It varies. Most of the time, there're a dozen of God's wonderful creatures living with me."

That probably meant there were more until Squeezy got

hungry. "How many dogs?" I asked, hoping to move the conversation closer to the reason for our visit.

She bit her lower lip, held out her hand and raised her fingers, one at a time. "Let's see, Bruce, Ink Spot, Little Dog, Pooch, Gink, and Lady. That's six today. Now don't neglect asking about my other lovely creatures."

"What're their names?" Mr. Nosy asked.

She pointed her cane at the boa. "You already met Squeezy. There are three cats, Cat One, Cat Two, and Crazy. My poor little parrot, Jolly Roger, must stay upstairs. He doesn't get along with the cats, and his vocabulary is, well let's say, his mouth needs to be washed out with soap more often than I would like. We celebrated his ninth birthday before I went to visit poor Tommy."

Charles wiggled his fingers like he was counting. "Martha, if my ciphering is right, that's only eleven pets. Didn't you say twelve?"

"Oh, you're right. I keep forgetting Davy Crockett." She looked around like Davy was loose in the room. I hoped Mr. Crockett wasn't another snake.

"Davy Crockett?" Charles said.

"A raccoon. He's my indoor/outdoor pet." She put her finger to her lips, and whispered, "It's illegal to have a raccoon as a pet. You won't turn me in to the pet police, will you?"

We assured her we wouldn't although turning her in to a mental institution was becoming a tempting option.

"Martha," I said. "Are any of your dogs Australian Terriers?"

"What a queer question, young man. Gink is."

Charles said, "Gink?"

"The word Gink means 'a peculiar fellow,' in Australian.

That's why Vincent and I named our little fellow that. That little bugger, Gink, not Vincent, was as strange as any dog we ever had."

Pot calling a kettle black came to mind.

"Vincent's not here is he?" Charles said.

"Heavens no. I dumped him back in Atlanta eons ago. Can you believe he hated the beach?"

"No, ma'am," Charles said.

"Now young men, don't get me wrong. Vincent was a wonderful husband, and we had some great times. I remember back when we got married in '58, and he bought the prettiest blue, 1957 Chevy. For our honeymoon, we drove all the way to the Grand Canyon, soaking in the air from the open windows. Gink would stick his head out the window and gobble up the breeze like he was lapping water. Ah, the good old days."

Now to get back to the not-so-good current days. "Martha, I'm confused. Gink was your Australian Terrier when you were in Atlanta?"

She nodded.

"Yet, when you were naming your dogs, didn't you say Gink?"

"Yes, so?"

"Gink is an Australian Terrier, right?"

She nodded again.

"And he's in the other room with your other dogs?"

Another nod.

"I see," I said, although I didn't. "How long have you had Gink?"

"Let's see. It was a few days before I left to visit poor Tommy. He had a stroke, you know?"

She had my attention. I leaned forward in the chair and motioned for her to continue.

"I was out back filling the food bowls. I put food out for the poor strays. Terrible how some people just throw their pets out to fend for themselves. Terrible. I was filling the bowls when the cutest little Australian Terrier peeked around the corner of the house. He saw the food and zip, he was eating out of the bowl. He was a spittin' image of Gink. Lo-and-behold, the poor thing didn't have a collar and licked my hand just like Gink used to do. Oh, the memories the cute thing brought back. Did I ever tell you about Vincent, Gink, and me going to the Grand Canyon?"

"Yes," I said.

She continued, "I simply had to bring him in, feed him, and give him a warm home to live in." She closed her eyes and slowly shook her head. "I had to."

I didn't know who I felt sorrier for, Martha or Dude. Martha was reliving her past through Gink, umm, Pluto, and we were here to shatter her memories. And, I can't imagine how much anguish Dude has been going though without Pluto. I also realized that Martha hadn't asked why two near strangers appeared at her door.

I was trying to figure out how to broach the subject of her taking Dude's dog. Charles, didn't share my dilemma.

He nodded toward the door separating us from the rest of her family. "Martha, what if I told you that Gink belongs to our friend, Dude Sloan?"

Her hand jerked up to cover her mouth. I would have sworn that Squeezy hissed at Charles. Martha exhaled and said, "Oh my heavens. That's not possible. Gink didn't have a collar. He came to me and begged me to take him in." She lowered her head. "Who's this Dude fellow?"

I explained who he was and how Pluto had escaped, caught his collar on something in the yard, and how Dude and several others had been looking for him for days. She appeared to be shrinking in her chair. It may have been the light, but I thought I saw tears in her eyes. Charles and I remained silent. That was the least we could do after ruining her day.

She pushed herself out of the chair and walked to the door where the dogs had been herded. She opened the door a few inches, bent down, and said, "Here, Gink."

Dude's look-alike inched his way through the door, saw Charles, jumped in his lap, and licked his face. Charles returned Pluto's "kisses" and said something to him in dog-speak.

Martha returned to her chair, and whispered, "What's his name?"

Charles gave his lap mate another kiss, and said, "Dude Sloan."

"No, what's Gink's name?"

"Pluto," I said.

"That's a funny name," said the person who has a snake named Squeezy, and cats named Cat One and Cat Two.

I explained how Dude was an astronomy buff and named his dog after the dwarf planet.

"He must be heartbroken," she said after a long, uncomfortable silence.

I said, "He is."

She stared at Pluto, and said, "You should call him and let him know his pup's safe. He can come get him."

"That's a good idea, Martha," I said.

"Won't you call him now? I feel horrible that I stole someone's family member. Horrible."

I punched in Dude's number in my phone, and was rewarded with, "Unless you know where Pluto is, I don't want to talk to you."

I smiled, told him who I was, and broke the news. Good news for Dude, not so good for Martha.

He screamed so loud that I moved the phone a foot away from my ear. He screamed a second time before I had the nerve to return the phone close enough to tell him where we were.

I heard Dude's 1970 Chevrolet El Camino a block before it pulled in Martha's drive. I opened the front door before he knocked it off the hinges. I'd never seen Dude move so quickly. Pluto ran a close second as he charged out of Charles's lap and met his master in the center of the room.

Watching Dude reunite with Pluto was a sight that would soften the hardest heart. I wouldn't call it a Christmas miracle, but it was close. Even Martha, who'd moments earlier been tearing up about losing Gink, and feeling badly about taking in someone else's dog, broke into a smile.

Charles had tears in his eyes.

I wasn't far behind.

Chapter 29

Charles and I left Martha, Dude, and Pluto/Gink after Martha apologized profusely for taking the surf shop owner's dog, and Dude told her, "Me be giggly getting Pluto back." He also told her that he wanted to meet all of Pluto's new four-, two-, and zero-legged friends. We would've stayed longer, but Dude told Martha that it'd "be cool" to wrap Squeezy around his neck. That was our cue to exit.

Charles dropped me at the house after saying he'd had enough excitement for one morning and wanted to take a nap to get ready for First Light's Christmas Eve service. A cold wave was pushing through the area since my early morning walk to the Dog. The sky morphed from chamber of commerce blue to threatening rain. I didn't need a nap yet thought spending several hours inside was becoming a better idea. I knew Dude would be so excited about getting Pluto back that he wouldn't think to let anyone know his dog had been found.

I called the Chief who answered with, "Ho, Ho, Ho!

Merry Christmas Eve. If you say anything to stomp on my feelings of great joy, you won't live long enough to wish anyone Merry Christmas tomorrow."

"Cindy, I'm about to make your day of feeling great joy even better."

"You and Charles are moving to Tibet."

"Guess again."

"You and Charles are moving to Tibet and taking my husband with you."

"What if I told you that Pluto has been reunited with Dude?"

"Has he?"

"Yes," I said, through a smile.

"Oh, my God. That's incredible. How, when, where?"

I filled her in on some details, leaving out the names of Martha's animals, my near snake-handling experience, and Martha's honeymoon trip to the Grand Canyon.

"Chris, that's the best news you could've given me. Thanks for letting me know."

"You're the first person I've called. I'll let you get back to whatever police chiefs do on Christmas Eve."

"Don't go so fast, bearer of great news. I have a kernel of news for you although it's not as great as Pluto's return. I talked to the landlord where Joy lives or lived before she moved here. The guy who sounds about as smart as a corkscrew, but not as useful, is on vacation in some town in Maryland I've never heard of. He thought it was a brilliant idea to leave his tenants in a lurch while he's frolicking with some floozy near our nation's capital."

"Did he tell you that's what he's doing?"

"Nah, he sounded like someone who'd be frolicking with a floozy. He remembered Joyce Tolliver, called her a 'hot chick' and said if he was twenty years older, or she was twenty years younger, he'd be camped out on her curb hoping she'd pick him up. Honest to God that's what he said. Yuck. I told him I wasn't a hot chick, but was a police chief and carried a gun, and if he didn't want me camped on his curb, he'd call the second he got back to the complex and let me in her apartment."

"What'd he say?"

"Yes, sir, Chief, ma'am."

"When's he coming back?"

"Day after Christmas."

"You'll call me when he gets back?"

"Nope. I'll be calling the tenant who's paid rent for that apartment. If she wants to let you know that's her business."

"Fair enough. Anything on the whereabouts of Taylor Strong?"

"Chris, you sure know how to drag a girl down after cheering her up about Pluto."

"Sorry."

"Our Mr. Strong has a rap sheet. If Preacher Burl was correct about his former resident attending school to learn locksmithing, either the school specialized in training burglars, or didn't check his background before letting him in."

"Is that what he'd been arrested for?"

"Yep, his career of crime had been given three years off when he was taking advantage of an all-expense paid vacation in Arkansas."

"Any idea where he is?"

"Nary a clue. I'm going to swing by the house this afternoon to see if the driver's license photo that was on record matches the Taylor Strong who stayed there. I'm fairly certain it will, but there's always the chance it's another guy with the same name."

"Anything more on his car?"

"Negative. If I learn anything, you might be one of the first I'll let know."

I knew not to push. "That'd be great, Cindy."

"Of course, it would."

My next call was to Preacher Burl.

"Brother Chris," he said, based on my name appearing on his phone, since I hadn't said anything.

"Yes, Preacher."

"Are you psychic?"

"Preacher, I've been accused of many things. That's not one of them. Why?"

"I was reaching for the phone to call you."

"Why were you going to call?"

"You called first. What do I owe the pleasure of this call?"

I shared the news about Pluto's reappearance, and Burl responded with "Hallelujah," and a prayer. I then told him that he would be receiving a visit from Chief LaMond and the reason for her visit.

"Ah, Brother Chris, perhaps you are psychic after all."

Burl was beginning to sound more and more like some of my other friends with disjointed comments, thoughts, and occasionally, actions. I asked what he meant.

"Brother Lawrence from Holy City Locksmiths returned my call less than an hour ago. That's the company I'd told Brother Taylor about. The store was closed today, but out of habit, Brother Lawrence checks his messages when the store's closed. He said that around Christmas it's not uncommon for people to get locked out of their home or vehicle. Mine happened to be the fifth message left for—"

"That's interesting, Preacher," I interrupted. "What did he say about Taylor?"

"He had little to share. It seems that Brother Taylor never showed for the interview. Can I surmise that Sister Cindy's visit is related to Brother Taylor's past?"

I told him what I knew about his former resident and the reason for Cindy's visit.

It took him a long time to say, "Brother Chris, I have a confession to make, and a dilemma that I face in my profession."

"What?"

"First, the dilemma. Faith is the foundation of my being. I, by personality and profession, seek the good in everyone. Over the years, I have seen firsthand how even the most horrid person can, as we preachers are prone to say, see the light. Men and women of all ilk can turn their lives around. I truly believe that miracles occur." He was silent for a moment, before repeating, "Miracles occur."

"That's wonderful, Preacher."

"There's a downside, which leads to my confession. When I opened Hope House, I did so with much trepidation. It was created as a place where those with little hope could find not only the necessities of a warm bed and a warm meal, but where they could find, as its name says, hope. From hopeless to hope requires change, a change in the residents. It's not up to me, nor is it in me to control the changes. That is up to a much higher power than in this humble, lowly, preacher man. Not everyone is ready or willing to make the necessary changes, hence the reason for my trepidation, and something that has kept me awake many a night with worry." He paused again. I started to ask him to elaborate, when he said, "I have no application for admittance. I have no way to determine where the potential resident is with his or her life; what black holes have existed in the past; and, what evil thoughts may be present. Brother Chris, I continually am in fear of introducing someone to the house who has evil intent. How, pray tell, is it fair to the others if I subject them to such a person?"

"Preacher, I've known you long enough to know that you'd do everything possible to prevent that from happening and look how much good Hope House has done. I know what Bernard was experiencing before you gave him a chance and hope. And look at Joy, she had no hope, nowhere to go. I don't know as much about Adrienne or Rebekah, but from what I see, you've helped them immensely."

"That may be true, Brother Chris. While it's taken me a long time to get to it, my confession is that I never had a good feeling about Brother Taylor."

"What about him?"

"I may not be all-knowing," he laughed. "Heavens, at times I'm not even part-knowing, but what I am decent at is detecting when someone is not being truthful. Brother Taylor often fit in that group. I should never have let him move in. I knew he was lying about previous jobs. That's one reason I was intent on him attending the job interview at Holy City Locksmiths. I figured if they liked him, they would check his background. If there was nothing in it to raise red flags, he'd get the job and be on the road to a productive life. Most everyone lies about something. I told myself that his could be minor and Hope House was giving him the break he needed."

"Preacher, you had no way of knowing. You shouldn't beat yourself up. You do wonderful work."

"Perhaps. I can only pray that by letting Brother Taylor reside here, it didn't contribute to what he did to Sister Joy."

"Preacher, he didn't meet her there. Whatever happened took place before she knew about your ministry."

"I suppose you're right. I must focus on tonight's message and not let this interfere with how I interact with those loyal members of my flock who will be celebrating Christmas Eve with fellow believers. You will be there tonight, won't you?"

"Of course," I said, like there could be any other option.

Chapter 30

The weather continued to deteriorate, so First Light's Christmas Eve service would be in the storefront location. Last Christmas, the service was in a tent on the beach, but the tent wasn't available this year.

Joy met me at the door and asked if we could talk after the service. I told her yes, and she joined Mary and her two girls in the second pew. I smiled as I remembered watching Mary, Joanie, and Jewel enter last year's Christmas Eve service. The girls had been wearing new clothes and entered the tent with their heads held high, radiating pride in their appearance.

Charles was in the third pew waving for me to join him. I passed Amber and her son, Jason, seated with Samuel and his dad. Amber nodded to me as I passed. I slid in beside Charles and watched Joy, Joanie and Jewel laughing. Mary hushed them.

Preacher Burl waved his hands for latecomers and those who wanted to continue their conversations to take their seats, and he began with, "Please silence thy portable communication devices." Tonight, it was followed by him encouraging us to make a joyful noise unto the Lord by singing "O Come All Ye Faithful."

We tried to sound joyful, but William Hansel had the lone true singing voice. Burl thanked us for coming and began his traditional Christmas Eve sermon. I had to give him credit, he'd overcome his earlier feelings of trepidation and guilt for allowing Taylor to stay in Hope House. His message was inspirational, heartwarming, and had the rapt attention of everyone present. He followed it with another carol, a reminder of tomorrow morning's regular Sunday service, before asking William to end the service with a solo of "Silent Night."

We slowly wandered out of the sanctuary into a light rain. Joanie asked her mom if the rain was going to turn to snow for Christmas. I didn't hear Mary's answer, but knew it would disappoint her daughter. Joy moved beside Charles and me. I asked if it was okay if Charles joined us. She said sure, and I suggested we make the short walk to the Crab Shack where we could stay dry and talk. Charles was leading the group, followed by Joy and me. As we got to the restaurant, I noticed a black car slowly pass us on Center Street and then turn on East Erie Avenue just past the restaurant. In the glow of the streetlight, it looked like it had a dent in the front bumper. Hadn't Bernard mentioned that Taylor's Ford Focus had a dent? Was the car that passed us a Focus or was I being paranoid? No way to know now.

The restaurant, normally crowded on Saturday nights, was near empty. A couple of others from the church service were seated near the bar, and a half-dozen patrons were scattered throughout the dining room. We were told to sit anywhere, and I suggested a table by the wall and away from others. The server appeared and asked what we wanted to drink. Joy asked what imported beers they had, the server told her, and Joy said Heineken. Charles said Bud, and I ordered the house wine.

"I remembered this morning that I preferred imported beer," Joy said, explaining her order.

"That's great," I said. "Anything else new?"

"That's what I wanted to talk about. Yesterday afternoon, your police chief came to talk to Preacher Burl. I didn't know the chief was there and walked in the kitchen where they were talking. I apologized and Chief LaMond said I wasn't interrupting. She had a driver's license photo and asked if I recognized the person."

"Did you?" Charles blurted, before Joy could finish talking.

She put both palms on the table and leaned forward. "It was him."

Charles said, "Who?"

"The man in the boat."

"You're certain?" I said.

She nodded, and said, "I remember walking home from work and the next thing I remember was laying on the back seat of the boat with my hands and feet tied. My head hurt so much that I figured I must still be alive. There was a dim light by the boat's steering wheel, and I recognized that man Taylor in the front seat. No doubt, it was him. It was dark in the rest of the boat and I never got a good look at the other guy. I already told you what happened next."

Drinks arrived, and the server asked if we wanted something to eat. Charles and I declined, and Joy asked me if she could borrow a few dollars. Charles said that she couldn't borrow anything and that he would pay. A Christmas miracle was in the making. She told the server that she wanted a cup of she crab soup and the house salad.

The server left, and I said, "Joy, do you remember anything else?"

"Not about them taking me out to dump me in the ocean. I remember my apartment in that building that you and I walked around. It came furnished, and I was traveling light. The only thing I had in there was a large suitcase and some hang-up clothes. Nothing more."

"Joy," I said, "did you tell Chief LaMond everything you remembered?"

She smiled for the first time since the service ended. "Everything but liking imported beer."

Charles said, "It sounds like a lot of your memory's back. Had you made friends in your apartment building or from the job at the bar?"

"Not really. I only worked at Blackbeard's two nights, and I hadn't lived much longer than that in the apartment. I nodded at a couple of other ladies who lived at the complex. I already have more friends here than over there or anywhere else I've lived."

Charles patted her on the arm, and said, "Folly folks are addictive."

I added, "You looked like you were enjoying sitting with Mary and her girls."

She smiled and sipped her beer. "The kids are adorable, and Mary actually stopped by yesterday to visit, to visit me. Can you believe that? She could be the daughter I never had." She hesitated, and turned to me, "Chris, Mary tells me that you helped her find a place to live after you discovered that she and her gals were sneaking in vacant rental houses to have somewhere to sleep."

"Several people helped Mary and her children. I didn't do more than anyone else."

Joy smiled. "That's not Mary's version."

I was embarrassed and changed the subject. "Will you be attending Cal's party tomorrow afternoon?"

"Preacher Burl said that it was an event I couldn't miss."

"More than going to church tomorrow morning?" Charles said.

She took another sip, smiled, and said, "Nope, he said the party was the second-best event happening on Folly tomorrow."

We watched Joy enjoying the soup and salad and talked more about what she remembered about the apartment and previously living in Atlanta. Her mood improved the more she recalled and recounted the past. She'd finished her meal and thanked Charles and me for an entertaining and happy evening. From our vantage point, it looked like the rain had stopped, and I suggested that it may be a good time for her to walk home.

Charles's home was in the opposite direction, so I told him to head to his apartment and I'd escort Joy home.

Chapter 31

Joy was euphoric on the way home. She hooked her arm in mine and kept talking about how much she enjoyed spending time with the others in Hope House. It was as if an anvil had been lifted off her shoulders. We were two houses from her place when a light drizzle filled the air. The house next to Hope had strands of multi-colored lights on large shrubs beside the drive. If I hadn't been looking at the Christmas lights, I would've missed a car backed to the rear of the neighbor's house—the same car that I would've sworn I'd seen on Center Street when Charles, Joy, and I were entering the Crab Shack. I was even more certain it was the same vehicle when the red and green Christmas lights reflected off a dented bumper.

I couldn't tell if anyone was in it without walking up the drive. Joy's safety was my main concern, so I pretended to not see the vehicle and continued walking her home. We started up the steps and she asked if I wanted to come in.

"Preacher Burl always has coffee brewing if you want some."

I opened the door and said, "That's a kind offer, but it's been a long day and I need to rest up for tomorrow's church service and Cal's party."

"I should do the same."

I told her to lock the door behind her. She said she would, and good to her word, I heard the tumbler secure the entry.

The rain had increased, and I wondered what to do. Should I approach the vehicle? Should I call the police? If the car belonged to the neighbor and had been there all night, I'd look foolish. I slowed as I crossed the drive where the car was parked. The lights reflected off the vehicle, but the rain-covered windshield, kept me from seeing if it was occupied. I decided to keep walking and regardless how foolish it may make me look, call the police as soon as I was out of sight from the suspicious vehicle.

I was startled to hear the car door slam shut and turned to see what was going on. A man wearing a black, hooded raincoat was heading toward me. My first thought was that it was Taylor Strong although I wasn't certain since the Christmas lights were the only illumination, and I'd only seen him twice. What I did know was that whoever it was gripped a baseball bat, and from his body language, knew how to use it.

Now what? Running wasn't an option. The man was three decades younger than me, and even when I was younger, I wasn't that fast. I probably outweighed him by thirty pounds and would have a chance, although slight, to subdue him in a fair fight. The bat and my age eliminated a fight being fair. It's amazing how much goes through your mind in a split second. My best option was to wait for him to swing at me and try to grab the bat's barrel before it contacted my body. With luck, it would throw him off balance and I might be able to wrestle him down or get the bat. *Might* being the key word.

I didn't have to put my feeble plan into action. I caught a glimpse of someone darting from beside the house and lunge at the bat-wielding assailant. The latest addition to the fray blindsided my attacker and collided with such force that both men were knocked to the concrete driveway. The bat flew in the opposite direction. I grabbed the weapon and stepped back from the men. I then I recognized it was Bernard who'd saved me from being a baseball. The man who was coming after me hadn't moved since he'd smacked into the drive. Bernard slowly pushed himself up and rubbed his elbow that had been under the other man when he struck the drive. The rain intensified, Bernard's hair was plastered to his head, and a wide smile was plastered to his face.

I stared at the assailant. He hadn't moved and must've been knocked out when his head hit the pavement. I reached for my phone to call the police and then heard the siren from a Folly Beach police cruiser less than a block away. The car stopped in front of the drive and Officer Allen Spencer rushed to the three of us.

Spencer glanced at Bernard, felt the unmoving person's neck for a pulse, and called for an ambulance. He then turned to me. "Mr. Landrum, I should have known. What's going on?"

"I walked Joy Tolliver to Hope House after supper." I pointed to the car. "I saw that car and was afraid it belonged to Taylor Strong, the man suspected of abducting Joy. I was going to call the police when a man—"

Bernard interrupted, "It's Taylor Strong, sir."

"Thank you," Spencer said, and turned back to me.

I continued with the story up to when Bernard jumped out of nowhere and collided with Taylor.

The rain continued to fall, and Spencer turned to Bernard. "Why were you out in this lousy weather and able to see what was happening?"

A fire engine arrived before Bernard could share his version of the event. One of Folly's EMT firefighters knelt beside Taylor. The other firefighter opened a large umbrella over his colleague and Taylor.

I said, "Officer Spencer, before Bernard answers, could we take this conversation inside? We'd be more comfortable out of the rain."

A second patrol car arrived, and Spencer told the new arrival to keep watch on the unconscious man.

Bernard led us to the door which was opened by Adrienne wearing a long, white robe and house slippers. She waved us in, hugged Bernard, and whispered to him, "Are you okay, hero?"

He told her that other than a sore elbow, he was fine, and followed the rest of us to the living room. Burl met us and asked if we wanted coffee. He acted like it was nothing unusual to entertain three soaked men, including a police officer and a man carrying a baseball bat. I said coffee sounded good, and Bernard and Spencer agreed. Joy had slipped in behind Burl and had a confused look on her face. I didn't blame her.

Spencer took a notebook from his jacket, wiped water

off the cover, flipped through a few pages, and said, "Bernard, let's start again, why were you out there?"

"Sir, folks living here are a family, not by blood, but still a family. Families stick together." He pointed to Joy who had taken a seat on the sofa. "Joy is the latest member. I knew you all were looking for Taylor Strong for what you thought he did to Joy."

Burl returned with a tray carrying three coffee mugs and Adrienne handed them to Bernard, Allen, and me.

Allen thanked her and asked Bernard to continue.

"You see, I knew what Taylor drove and thought I saw it cruisin' past the house a couple of times earlier tonight. I wasn't sure it was him, so I didn't say anything. I took a little walk before it started to rain hard and saw the car back in the drive where it is now. It didn't belong to the owner of that house. Sir, that made me more than a mite suspicious. I went around the house and sneaked behind those shrubs out there. The driver was still in the car and not moving. I figured he was waiting to see where Joy was and maybe try to take or kill her." He stopped and caught his breath.

"How long were you there?" Spencer asked.

"I don't have a watch. I'd guess a half hour or so. I also don't have a phone, so I couldn't call for you to come check it out. Sir, I was afraid to leave and not see what the man in the car, umm, Taylor, was going to do. The rain got harder and harder."

"You had to be miserable," Burl added.

"Nah," Bernard said, "I did a lot of recon in Afghanistan, like hours at a time. A half hour in the rain was nothing."

Spencer said, "Then what happened?"

"I saw Mr. Landrum, umm, Chris, walking Joy to the

house. I was afraid Taylor was going to try to get her before she got in. He didn't, so I figured he was going to wait until everyone was asleep and do something then. I was surprised when Chris left, and Taylor went after him with a bat."

Spencer smiled for the first time, and said, "So, you took a football tackle to a baseball game."

Laughter, probably fueled by the release of tension more than Spencer's joke, filled the room.

Bernard added to the laughter, and then said, "Couldn't have said it better, sir."

"Allen," I said, "Were you headed here?"

Adrienne answered for the officer. "I called the police. Bernard thought he was hiding, maybe he was from Taylor, but I saw him behind the shrubs from my second-floor window. I remembered what he'd said about Taylor's car so when I saw it parked out there, I called the police. Bernard's right, we're a family, and I didn't want to see Joy, Bernard, or any of us hurt."

I heard the siren from an ambulance approaching and Allen jotted down Adrienne and Bernard's full name and asked Bernard if he wanted the EMTs to check his arm. Bernard said it was fine, and Allen asked if anyone had anything to add. None of us did.

Chapter 32

After last night's events, I was tempted to skip First Light's Christmas service. I'd told Preacher Burl and Joy that I'd be there, so I resisted temptation and walked to church. The rain that'd made last night more miserable than it had already been, was gone and nary a cloud could be seen.

I arrived fifteen minutes before I knew Preacher Burl would repeat his "Please silence thy portable communication devices" opening. A familiar group of people were gathered around the coffee urn at the front of the room. Charles was talking with Bernard. Joy, Adrienne, and Rebekah were huddled together in deep conversation, and William was talking with Dixie and Martha.

Charles spotted me at the entry and pointed to his wrist, his way of telling me that I was late. I shook my head, and he mouthed, "Just kidding."

The Christmas spirit had taken hold of my friend. I nodded to Lottie who was helping Burl with his robe.

Everyone wore their Christmas best, even Charles, who wore a solid red, long-sleeve sweatshirt instead of one featuring college logos. Burl headed to the lectern and Mary, Joanie, and Jewel entered and looked around. Joy spotted them and asked if they wanted to sit with her. In unison, Joanie and Jewel said, "Yes, oh yes." Mary ceded to their wishes, and the four moved to the second pew.

Barb entered as Burl was beginning his opening. She tiptoed to the back pew where I was sitting with Charles and squeezed my hand as she sat. "Sorry I'm late. I was at the store straightening up after being busy yesterday and lost track of time."

I saw fatigue in Burl's eyes, but he didn't let it show. His message was uplifting, his enthusiasm for, and telling about, the birth of Jesus was contagious, and miracle of miracles, the congregations singing of traditional Christmas carols, sounded good—okay, passable.

Before the closing song, Charles leaned my way and whispered, "Whenever I have a problem, I sing. Then I realize my singing is a lot worse than my problem."

"Did a President say that?"

"No, I did. Didn't you just hear me?"

William Hansel singing "What Child is This" drowned out more silliness from Charles.

Most of those in attendance appeared to want to linger in the sanctuary after the service. Burl said there was more coffee and a few of us took advantage of it.

Charles took me by the arm and moved to a corner of the room, and in a muffled voice, said, "Why did I hear about last night from Bernard and not from my best friend?"

"Charles, I was exhausted and the only thing I wanted

to do was go to sleep. Sorry."

Instead of berating me, he said, "Are you okay?"

The phone rang before I could assure him that I was. The screen read Cindy.

"Merry Christmas, Chief."

"Caller ID strikes again. Can you talk?"

I said for her to give me a second and walked outside where I'd have more privacy. Charles followed me. To keep him from flailing his arms and pointing to the phone, I put it on speaker and told Cindy to go ahead.

"Figured you'd want to know. Your new friend, the baseball batter, ain't what crooks call a stand-up guy. My guys turned him over to the Sheriff's Office when they got to the hospital. The detective called me a little while ago and said that it wasn't fifteen minutes after he started interrogating Taylor before he blamed everything on Raymond Tilford, his partner in crime. According to Taylor, it was Tilford's idea to burglarize the jewelry store, abduct Joy, steal the boat, take her out and dump her in the ocean. He didn't say it, but I suspect if given a chance, he'd blame Raymond for global warming, fighting in the Middle East, and shingles."

"Did he say why he attacked me?"

Cindy chuckled. "It appears that your surveillance skills aren't as good as your detective friend Charles."

Charles smiled, but kept his mouth shut. For once.

"And?" I said.

"Taylor thought he saw you looking at his car when you walked by with Joy, and when you were leaving, he said you slowed down and gazed his way. He figured he had to stop you before you did something stupid like calling the cops. Your reputation for nosing in my business, has spread to the criminal element. Tell Charles he needs to give you some lessons in surveilling."

"Never," I said.

Cindy laughed, and Charles stuck his lower lip out and pouted.

I asked, "Did Taylor tell them where to find Tilford?"

"Yep, and before you ask, they picked him up late last night and found some pretty earrings, necklaces, and watches in his car. Funny how they all were in boxes with Grogan's Fine Jewelry on the top."

"Cindy, thanks for letting me know. You still plan to go to Cal's party this afternoon?"

"Only if Charles, that idiotic, moronic, weird friend of yours isn't there." She then laughed.

"I'm not those things," Charles said.

Cindy said, "I know, you're not idiotic and moronic. Merry Christmas, Charles."

Charles said, "I'll admit to weird. How'd you know I was listening?"

"Charles, I'm the Chief. I know everything. Besides, do you think I don't know when a phone's on speaker? The only person Chris puts the phone on speaker for is his nosy friend. Merry Christmas to both of you, and bye."

———

Cal had said that this party would be bigger and better than ever. From the sounds coming from the room as I opened the door, he was right. Loud conversations mixed with laughter were coming from all corners. Christmas lights twinkled from the bar, the front of the stage, and from four trees.

Cal was in the center of the room standing beside a table holding bowls of salsa, avocado dip, and something with lettuce, tomatoes, and onions in it. Two bowls overflowed with chips. The smiling host wore his much-travelled, rhinestone-covered coat, red jeans, and his Stetson with twinkling lights around the crown. He was talking with Amber and her son while Samuel and his dad were scooping dip on a paper plate full of chips.

Gene Autry's 1950 version of "Frosty the Snowman" was playing on the Wurlitzer.

Charles leaned on the bar and was talking with Joy, Mary and her girls. Joy saw me at the door and waved for me to join her. I did, and Charles said that he was telling the ladies about the police catching the second person responsible for Joy's abduction. Bernard joined us, and Charles started the story over again. He was swinging his arm around. I was afraid he was going to slosh beer on Bernard from the bottle in his hand.

Adrienne and Rebekah had been standing in a corner by themselves, but slowly came our way after they saw that Bernard had joined the group. They each put an arm around Bernard and called him their hero. He turned three shades of red and looked at the floor. That made the ladies squeeze harder. Jim Reeves was singing "Silver Bells" and Adrienne hummed along while she was squeezing their embarrassed housemate.

Speaking of squeezing, Dixie and Martha peeked in the door, and hesitated before getting enough courage to enter. I nodded to Charles and then at the ladies. Charles took the hint and moved to greet them. I saw him get each a beer from the tub next to the appetizer table and they moved to the far side of the room.

Joy watched them go, and leaned close to me and said, "You won't believe this. Preacher Burl talked to Cal about me. Cal told him he had a powerful need for another bartender, that's how he said it, *powerful need*. Cal hired me, and Preacher Burl said I could stay at Hope House as long as I want to. Isn't that wonderful?"

It was, and I told her so.

Dude was next to stick his head in the door. Correction, Pluto stuck his head in and then Dude. Pluto sniffed the air like he knew there must be a hamburger nearby with his name on it. Martha saw Pluto and left Dixie and Charles standing before she scooped up the canine and gave it a series of kisses.

I excused myself from Joy and moved toward Pluto, hopefully to prevent a war over the canine suffering an identity crisis. I hadn't needed to. Dude stood back, smiled, and told Martha that she could visit Pluto any time.

She thanked him, and added, "Can I call him Gink?"

"That be cool. His official name now be Pluto Gink Sloan."

Barb entered wearing a red sweater without any Christmas message adoring it, and came over to me and kissed my cheek and said, "Want to hunt shark teeth in the morning?"

"No," I said, so loud that two people standing nearby stopped talking and stared at me.

Burl was next to arrive. He wore a Santa hat and a sweater that would win any ugly Christmas sweater contest. He made his way around the room patting people on the back, kissing ladies on the cheek, and lifting and hugging Joanie and Jewel.

Cal saw Burl and moved close and whispered something

to him. Burl shook his head so hard that the Santa hat nearly fell off. Cal smiled, patted the preacher on the back, and moved to the stage in front of the room. He waited for Brenda Lee to finish "Rockin' Around the Christmas Tree," and unplugged the jukebox.

He clinked two beer bottles together close to the antique mic that he's sung approximately a trillion songs in over the years. "Yo! How about lending me an ear?"

All but Dixie and Martha stopped talking. Cal tried again and this time they stopped and turned to the country singer.

Cal tipped his Stetson to the group. "Merry Christmas. This is our biggest Christmas shindig ever. Thanks for coming and joining this old crooner on his favorite day of the year. Now, I've got a question. How many of you'd like to hear Preacher Burl and me sing a duet?"

All but Burl responded by either clapping or saying, "Yes." Burl stared at the floor and shook his head.

"That's what I thought," Cal said. "If you were here last Christmas, I bet you remember the preacher and me singing, 'Silent Night.' I know I do. Come on up, Preacher."

Burl glanced at the door leading outside. I suspected that's where he'd rather be, but in the spirit of Christmas, he slowly moved to the stage while Cal grabbed his guitar. Burl faked a smile and moved to the mic like he would approach a rattlesnake. Cal whispered something to Burl and Burl responded.

Cal stepped to the mic and pulled Burl closer. "Gals and guys," the singer said, "I can't think of a better song to sing than this one. Here's to you, Joy, my newest bartender, and another fine addition to our community."

They began singing "Joy to the World," and two minutes later ended with,

"He rules the world with truth and grace,
And makes the nations prove
The glories of His righteousness,
And wonders of his love,
And wonders of his love."

About the Author

Bill Noel is the best-selling author of fifteen novels in the popular Folly Beach Mystery series. Besides being an award-winning novelist, Noel is a fine arts photographer and lives in Louisville, Kentucky, with his wife, Susan, and his off-kilter imagination. Learn more about the series, and the author by visiting www.billnoel.com.

Made in the
USA
Middletown, DE

76499713R00129